WILD MOON

KINGDOM OF WOLVES

C.R. JANE
MILA YOUNG

CONTENTS

DEDICATION

For every girl whose gotten lost and along the way found their wild...

JOIN OUR READERS' GROUP

Stay up to date with C.R. Jane by joining her Facebook readers' group, C.R.'s Fated Realm. Ask questions, get first looks at new books/series, and have fun with other book lovers!

Join C.R. Jane's Group
www.facebook.com/groups/C.R.FatedRealm

$\approx$

Join Mila Young's Wicked Readers Group to chat directly with Mila and other readers about her books, enter giveaways, and generally just have loads of fun!

Join Mila Young's Group
www.facebook.com/groups/milayoungwickedreaders

KINGDOM OF WOLVES SERIES

FROM C.R. JANE AND MILA YOUNG

Wild Moon

Wild Heart

Wild Girl

These stories are set in the Kingdom of Wolves shared world, but our Wild series will follow Rune's continuing story with her alphas.

WILD MOON

REAL WOLVES BITE...

I was taught my whole life about the importance of true mates, how when you find that one wolf for you, everything falls into place.

Everyone who taught me that was a liar.

When I found my true mate, happily ever after sure as hell didn't start, but hell definitely began.

I ran away, and now I've been searching for peace for weeks as I drive around the country.

I didn't mean to take the wrong road.

I didn't mean to make it to that small town.

And I didn't mean to meet two men, who set me and my wolf on fire.

But here I am somehow, and peace is the last thing I've found.

And don't forget about the serial killer...

I was cursed.

That had to be it.

I'd come to this conclusion somewhere on the highway, lost in the middle of nowhere, in a strip of land so empty and so flat, it made you feel like you were the only person on the planet. Hours after my car had been broken into while I used the restroom, leaving me with only a twenty-dollar bill to my name.

I'd been driving for weeks…or was it months already? And the only conclusion for why my life had thus far been a giant shit show of the most epic proportions was because I was cursed.

I was perhaps also an idiot.

The sun was falling in the west, and the sky was a kaleidoscope of color. A mixture of pinks and reds that at one point, would have made me shed a tear, back when I had a heart that could still be affected by beautiful things.

Alistair had sucked all the beauty out of my life, twisted and tore at my heart until it was incapable of viewing the world as it once had.

And yet something inside of me, something that was irrevocably tied to him for forever, it still missed him. Despite what he had done, what he'd kept from me. Despite the fact that I'd been told my whole life how wonderful my life was going to be once I found my true mate, and then he promptly destroyed any notions of happily ever after I'd ever dreamed about.

Despite all of that, I still wanted him.

And I always would. Because that's how true mates worked. It was a bond that forced you to need something, even if it would kill you.

Hence why I was thinking that I was cursed.

I dragged myself away from my pity party as the sun finally sank below the horizon. The landscape was changing around me. Jagged rocks were springing up from the land that I'd sworn had been flat as a board just a few minutes ago. Had I been lost in my head for that long? That wouldn't have been a surprise since I'd spent most of the last few weeks stuck in my head. I really needed to pay attention every once in a while though.

The landscape was definitely getting higher and higher, and I could see even steeper peaks up ahead. The road in front of me winded up through them. And now the sun was officially gone, and the stars were peaking their way out in the velvet sky.

Did I mention I was terrified of heights? And not just heights, add in driving and the dark too, and you officially had the trifecta of ridiculous fears that I'd developed over the years.

For a moment, I contemplated pulling over to the side of the road and trying to sleep until the morning. I quickly shook that thought away.

Despite the fact that a part of me wanted to be with Alistair, my true mate, desperately, all the other parts wanted to make sure we never saw that asshole again. The large majority of my parts also wanted to live, and Alistair would kill me after what I'd done. I knew that for a fact.

Taking a deep breath, I continued to drive, and it just kept getting darker and darker.

There were no lights out here, of course there wasn't. Because why put lights in the middle of nowhere? I put my brights on, not giving a fuck. If I was going to drive through a mountain range in the pitch black, you better believe I was going to be able to see while doing it.

Looking in my rearview mirror, I began to freak when I saw headlights approaching. Any time I saw another car, I wondered if it was Alistair, if somehow, he'd found me despite the crazy precautions I'd taken to be hidden from him. Like the way I'd snuck a stash of cash from Alistair's safe and bought a car with it when I was supposed to be grocery shopping. The way I'd used more of that cash to pay for everything I'd done on this road trip from hell. The way I'd gotten rid of my cell phone when I left so there was no way he could track it. The way I'd been wearing an ebony wig twenty-four-seven to try and change my looks.

I breathed a bit easier when I saw it was a Honda Accord. Alistair wouldn't be caught dead in a car that didn't scream money and privilege. While I was all about the practicality and the gas mileage of a Honda, Alistair wouldn't get in one no matter the circumstances, even if it was the only way to catch me.

My breathing increased however as the terrain began to rapidly ascend and I realized I was no longer approaching the mountain, I was going up the motherfucker.

There was a guardrail off to my right, but that didn't calm me down. I was now hyperventilating as I white-knuckled the steering wheel and leaned forward, trying to make sure I stayed right on that white line. If I was on that white line, then I wouldn't go off the edge. Right?

A loud honk had me jumping in my seat, swearing, and swerving the car. I hadn't handled unexpected things with grace over the last few years...but could I really be blamed for that after all that had happened?

I tore my eyes off the white line and glanced in the rearview, only to see that there were now a few cars lined up behind me. The driver behind me seemed to be waving his hands around.

Whoops. A glance at my speedometer showed that I was going about ten miles per hour right now. I highly doubted that was the speed limit, based on the cacophony of angry honks I was beginning to hear.

I rolled down my window, continuing to keep my eyes on that white line since my brain was filled with images of my car tumbling down the side of the mountain and bursting into flames fit for an action movie. I began to wave my arm out the window, trying to get them to go around me. Was there etiquette for this? Besides the obvious move of not driving forty miles under the speed limit.

The car behind me finally got the hint, and it swerved around me, honking loudly and rudely as it did so.

"Jerk," I muttered. The rest of the cars followed their leader, their brittle horns filling the night.

And then finally, it was just me.

Which maybe I hadn't been thinking through, because now that there weren't any other angry drivers to worry about, I was more aware than ever that I was painfully alone.

"What will it be like, Mama? When I find him," I whispered

to my mother as she curled up beside me on the bed, a copy of Harry Potter *laying in her lap just as it was every night.*

"He'll make all your dreams come true, baby," she said with a gentle smile. "He'll see all the parts in your heart, and he'll accept them no matter what he finds."

"Why are there different parts in my heart?" I asked, the six-year-old me very confused about the words my mother was saying.

She giggled in that magical way of hers, and I watched entranced at the love I could see in her eyes. Was every mother that wonderful?

"I just mean, sweetheart, when you find him, you'll feel complete," she said sweetly as she brushed a piece of hair out of my eyes.

"Did you feel complete when you met Daddy?" I asked, sadness creeping down my throat at the blurry memory of a man as big as a bear who always smelled like peppermint and those cigarettes he used to smoke constantly as he anxiously paced around the room.

Something in my mother's eyes flickered and changed. There was a look there that I didn't recognize, but which made my little heart uncomfortable because it was so unfamiliar from the gentle looks my mother always gave me.

"Do you promise it will be like that?" I spit out, suddenly desperate for that look in her eyes to go away and for her to give me the reassurance I could always expect from her.

"I promise," she whispered, that look in her gaze fading slowly away.

I settled back into my pillows, ready to hear what Harry, Ron, and Hermoine were up to next, confident that the future was bright because my mother had said so.

Too bad my mother turned out to be a liar.

"Holy shit," I screeched, swerving out of the lane as

something black...and furry, sprinted across the dim light of my headlights, startling me out of my journey to the past where I had no business spending time in the middle of the night in the freaking mountains.

"What the hell was that?" I whispered as I slowed down even more and tried to look around.

An even larger furry beast suddenly sprinted in front of my car, and this time, I yanked the steering wheel way too far to try not to hit it.

I screamed as my car went flying past that white line and careened off the embankment, the guardrails nowhere to be found. I went a few feet as I frantically pressed on the brake, those visions of my car tumbling down the mountains suddenly coming true right before my very eyes.

Was this how it ended? A sucktastic life ending with a fall down a mountain in the middle of nowhere.

Only me.

Shrubs and small trees...combined with my braking power, succeeded in slowing down my car, but the pine tree on the edge of the thick forest in front of me succeeded in stopping me completely. I choked on a scream as I hit the tree. The impact sending me flying forward as the airbags burst out of the steering wheel and door. I hadn't hit the tree very fast, but the force of the airbags sent me backwards, my neck whiplashing as it snapped back. The airbags ripped at my skin, burning my forearms, and a noxious plume of gas filled the air.

The silence after the crash was deafening for a long moment. But then a loud buzzing filled my ears as the adrenaline crashed against my veins. I coughed, wearily trying to wave my hand around to clear the air, the enormity of what had happened settling over my skin.

"Fuck," I gasped out. The human mind was truly exceptional. I mean, the fact that it could feel a myriad of emotions all at once as I was now.

Incredible.

"No, no, no," I cried out as I hit at the airbag and steering wheel in front of me.

My head and neck were beginning to hurt the longer I sat there, and a glance at my arms showed me that I did indeed have burns and lacerations from the stupid, fucking airbags.

"Okay, you can figure this out," I coached myself as I quit beating at my steering wheel and turned my attention to unlocking my seatbelt, which judging by the pain I felt in my chest, had definitely stopped me from flying through the windshield.

Small mercies.

After the seatbelt was successfully dismantled, I struggled against the car door, the movement sending agony against my protesting muscles. *This is why you shouldn't live on gas station snacks and fast food for weeks on end*, I thought to myself. *Maybe it wouldn't be so hard to open a small thing like a car door if my muscles actually existed in my arms anymore.*

Success! The car door finally flew open, and I promptly fell out of my seat into the shrubs and rocks that were waiting for me just outside. Apparently, my legs weren't working anymore.

I shivered as I looked around. Somehow, my lights were still working, and the area around me was eerily illuminated.

There was a thick forest just ahead of me. And although I couldn't see anything...it felt like something was watching me.

I shivered again and decided it was best to try and get to the road and see if I could flag someone down for help.

Although really, that was probably worse than staying here by the trees. I'd seen the news, I knew the danger of trying to hitchhike, especially out in the middle of nowhere like this. With my luck, I'd get picked up by a mugger or a murderer...or even Alistair. And not to mention those two animals I'd seen...

I groaned and reached back into the car to grab the tiny flashlight from my door that I'd picked up at...you guessed it...a gas station, and then I limped my way back towards the road, which was a seriously difficult task since I'd fallen down a shallow embankment. The roots, rocks, and weeds didn't exactly help. I was not a hiker. I was only a few feet away from the road when a howl ripped through the air. I stopped in my tracks. That thing inside of me that had been there for as long as I could remember perked up at the sound. There was a time that a wolf's howl meant home. A time that I believed my howl would once call out into the night. My mother had promised that it would be a moment I would remember forever.

That was just another one of her lies.

Although I'd once welcomed the howl of a wolf, right now, the sound was a reminder that I was in the wilderness and there was a real possibility that I could be eaten. There weren't any shifters out here, I'd seen the map many times as Alistair tried to plan world domination or whatever it was that he was interested in. Which meant the howl I was hearing was not a good sign.

Fuck, I sighed. I really was cursed. Deciding to proceed with my plan, I finally made it to the roadway, praying the next car that came by didn't contain a psychopath. I'd definitely already had my fair share of those.

I waited.

And I waited.

And I waited some more.

How was it I couldn't get cars off my ass earlier, and here I was, actually wanting cars to be on my ass, and they were nowhere to be seen? Had I taken a wrong turn somehow and stumbled upon a road that no one went down? I squinted at the road, trying to see if it looked like it was in disrepair. I hadn't noticed any out of the ordinary bumps.

"Are you fucking kidding me right now?" I screamed at the night sky, cursing at it for what felt like the millionth time.

Sighing and deciding I was going to just have to walk off this mountain myself, I set off down the dark road.

Weren't the stars supposed to be brighter out here? Where was the freaking moon?

I stumbled over a rock and barely caught myself with my hands. Of course, catching myself meant scraping my palms on the coarse asphalt and dropping my flashlight.

"Shit," I whispered, picking myself up and cradling my hands against me as the pain shot through me.

And there was a wolf howl again.

Perfect.

I'm sure the smell of my bloody palms was going to get me eaten alive.

Wouldn't that just be the most ironic way to go...ever.

I snorted, hysterical laughter threatening to spew from my mouth. I was definitely losing my mind.

Something shifted across the road just then, and I froze, the threat of laughter abruptly coming to a screeching halt.

I picked up my flashlight and began to jog down the road, despite the fact that I knew you were never supposed to run from a predator.

Where were all the fucking cars?

When nothing attacked me from behind, my confidence

grew and I started to run faster, despite the fact that my legs were screaming in protest.

I came to a halt when a road that diverted from the main one I'd been running on appeared in front of me just a ways off. I hesitated and tried to squint farther down the main road. I should just stay on this road, right?

The sound of something running down the main road seemingly straight towards me made the decision for me, and I darted down the roadway and quickly realized that it was going downhill rather than uphill as the highway had headed. That was a good sign I thought.

I sighed again as I slowed down to a quick walk, the effects of the crash and my extremely poor diet over the last few weeks doing me in. If I had to run again because something was after me, I was probably going to have to accept it.

Damn those Cool Ranch Doritos.

The air was freezing here. I had on a stained *I Love New Mexico* shirt I'd found in one of my convenience store runs. It was pink, so I knew I had to have it. Alistair had hated pink, banned it from my wardrobe in fact...

Was it going to last forever, this way that my heart would squeeze every time I thought of him? How was it possible to hate someone with every fiber of your being but still feel like you couldn't breathe without them?

I stifled a sob, determined not to cry for him.

"Never again," I whispered to myself, even as his face appeared in my mind as I remembered the way he'd been looking at me right before he ripped my world into a million pieces that had no hope of ever being put back together.

I was so lost in my four hundred and twentieth pity party that it took me a while to notice the lights beginning to pop up in the distance and the enormous wooden sign with the symbol of what looked like a wolf carved above a scrawled 'Welcome to Amarok.'

Amarok? What kind of name was that? And why hadn't I seen this on the map I'd poured over before setting off today?

I pushed myself to go faster, the lights giving me hope, even if I was wary of getting so close to civilization. The places I'd picked had been out in the middle of nowhere. Small inns and motels where drifters and vagabonds passed through, perfect for a girl on the run. Alistair was a big fan of the Four Seasons, so the places I'd picked were, again, perfect for avoiding detection.

Another howl sounded through the night, and I decided that going near people, and hopefully getting help for my car, was a much better outcome than the possibility of getting eaten alive.

I already knew what a wolf's bite felt like, and it wasn't an experience I wanted to repeat...

The buildings loomed larger as I got closer, and I wondered again how a town this size hadn't been on my map. I was pretty sure the map was up to date. A GPS on a phone would obviously have been more useful, but beggars couldn't be choosers.

I tried to look for a building where I could find help, but everything looked shut down for the night. Finally, I spotted a sign advertising a place called The Lair Inn. The walls were made of cobblestone, like something you'd find in a Brother's Grimm tale. For an inn, it seemed pretty deserted. I couldn't see anyone else around. Only the splash of water from a river nearby and the rustle of leaves filled the night. For moments, I couldn't help but wonder if I'd stumbled into a ghost town. But ghost towns didn't have pristine roads and building lights, so I guessed I could strike that possibility off the list, right?

The faint sound of a scream caught on the breeze from the woods behind me. Had I really heard that, or was it an animal cry?

I twisted around, my heart in my throat, and I stared into

the unbelievable darkness, seeing nothing. It didn't stop my imagination from picturing wolves looming in the shadows, about to lunge and kill me. The fact that I was a wolf shifter didn't stop wild wolves from attacking.

Today had been a terrible day, and I'd had my fair share of crap in my life. I'd come too far though to add death to my list of how much my situation currently sucked.

I whipped back around and sprinted the last few steps towards the inn, the hairs on my nape standing at attention. Panic flared in my chest as I got the distinct feeling that someone was watching me right at that moment. I plunged into the light hanging over the arched, wooden door and turned my back to the building. Part of me half expected something to be right on my heels, but there was nothing there. Just a lawn with wooden benches and tables. Still, my heart beat furiously fast.

Keep your shit together, I ordered myself.

It was bad enough I crashed my car, and now I was stuck in the middle of nowhere. But I couldn't let panic get the better of me.

Where the heck am I, anyway?

Wherever I'd arrived, I doubted Alistair would track me down right away, and I craved a warm bed desperately. Anything to be away from the dark woods and the feeling of being watched.

Not waiting another moment, I turned and pushed open the inn's door. The hinges creaked, announcing my entrance. Not that there was an audience to welcome me. The main bar area stood empty.

No music.

No fire burning.

Just an eerie silence at first.

I took a deep breath, inhaling a strong lemon scent like

the entire room had been plunged in Lysol. Not for the first time, I longed for the abilities that should have been mine. I could have scented the whole room, gotten a clear lay of the place. For a wolf, emotions had clear scents. It was just too bad I would never get to experience that firsthand.

Someone cleared their throat just then, and I jumped, realizing I wasn't alone in the room. I looked over and saw a middle-aged man now standing behind a long wooden counter. We stared at each other, and he cocked his head as he studied me. I saw his nostrils flare a few times, almost like he was trying to smell me.

That was odd.

My thoughts flew in a dozen directions all within the span of a microsecond. Would he hurt me? Even as the thought cycled through my mind, I knew it was crazy. Not every person of the male variety was a psychopath. But I couldn't help it.

I backed up a few steps, my first instinct to find an escape route, even though I had nowhere to escape to. My skin chilled with the notion I'd just made a terrible mistake coming here.

"Um...I-I better go. Sorry—"

"You look like you could do with a warm drink, maybe something to eat," the man said, a hint of uncertainty lacing his voice. His gaze skipped over my shoulder to the night outside, as if he feared what lingered in the woods too. His attention swept over my arms, seeing the blushing redness of the burns from the airbags.

I didn't move at first as the breeze from outside swished through my hair, curling around my body. I shivered with a sudden cold.

"You just arrived in town?"

When I looked closer, I saw there was softness in his

eyes, similar to how I'd remembered my mother's looking. That didn't bode well for my trust issues with this man.

"It's best not to wander through these woods late at night. It can be a dangerous place."

He turned to collect a tall glass from the shelves behind him, acting purposely nonchalant, as if he knew how close to the edge I was in completely losing it.

I really didn't want to go back out there alone. Not when I was sure something had been stalking me.

I would just stay awhile, I decided as I continued to watch him closely for any sudden movement, at least to find out where I was and where to stay for the night.

I shut the door, closing out the breeze, and walked toward the long bar against the back wall, taking in the room. Small round tables and chairs peppered half of it, wine barrels decorated the side wall, and a massive, stone fireplace sitting in shadows adorned the other. A closed door sat to my far left and another behind the bar.

Wooden chandeliers decorated with small carvings of bears and mountain lions flickered overhead. There was a quaintness about the place, and a strangeness at the same time that I couldn't put my finger on. It was pretty late, so I guessed that explained why there were no guests milling around, but still...it felt strange.

"I got into an accident just off the main road," I admitted and took a seat on a round stool.

"You walked all the way here in the dark? Are you injured?" he asked, turning toward me and filling my glass with ice.

"Just some water please," I asked, parched from the long walk. "I think I'm all right, but it was quite a hike."

Around us, photographs of the beautiful forest land-scapes dotted the wooden walls. Realizing I was still holding onto the flashlight, I set it near the stool just as a chilled glass of water landed on the bar in front of me.

"Thank you." I didn't wait and drank the whole thing in seconds, the chilled water racing down my throat. Then I looked up at the man. He was older than I'd first assumed, with silvery short hair and piercing dark eyes. His short smile tugged his ears outward slightly and gave him an almost approachable feel. He was on the slim side, and the checkered, short-sleeved top he wore hung loosely on him.

"I'm Jim and I run The Lair with my wife, Carrie. She's gone to bed early tonight, she takes the morning shift." From across the bar, he bent forward and rested his elbows on the counter, close enough to see the deep lines at the corners of his eyes, the white strands in his bushy eyebrows, the flicker of friendliness in his gaze that I wasn't used to seeing.

No one had been friendly to me in a very long time... besides Nelly.

I couldn't think about her.

"Now, you can take one of the rooms upstairs for the night if you want. We don't get many tourists in this area, so with the kitchen shut, all I can offer you is a grilled cheese sandwich. So while I make that, how about you tell me where you broke down on the main road so we can get you back on your way tomorrow?"

For a second, I was back behind the steering wheel about to hit the tree.

Bang.

I shuddered in my skin.

I mentally shook away the image and focused on Jim, who pushed open the door behind the bar and entered a small kitchen. He left it open so I had direct line of sight to him, a move I appreciated. A warm bed sounded perfect, but was it safe? Did I have a choice?

You always have a choice. Nelly's voice echoed in my ears. She was the eldest female in Alistair's pack, and the only one really to care about me. She'd always impart small words of wisdom when no one was looking our way, including telling me I needed to try and leave Alistair...and then helping me make that happen.

Glancing up at Jim, who was buttering the slices of bread, adding cheese, and placing it onto the grill, I said, "I hit a tree not too far from the turn off coming into this town. But there's no one outside. At first, I thought I stumbled across an abandoned town." My attempt to smile came out lopsided from disuse, but thankfully, he wasn't looking my way.

"You're in Amarok, dear. A place where anyone is welcome and your business is your own. Most folk keep to themselves, and like I said, the woods at night are not safe." He stepped out of the kitchen and set the plate with the grilled cheese sandwich in front of me, then went back to wiping the glasses on the sink behind him.

I collected the sandwich and bit into it, melting into my seat at how hungry I'd been, his words running through my mind. A town where people minded their own business? The idea intrigued me. With it came a calmness I hadn't felt in weeks...months...years.

But I'd also learned the hard way that nothing was ever as it first appeared.

It wasn't long before I finished my meal and Jim showed me upstairs to my bedroom. He was a man of few words, and once he shut the door, I locked myself inside.

A bed with a floral blanket, dresser, table, and chairs by

the window. It was simple. A far cry from the lavish sheets I'd slept on at Alistair's.

It was perfect.

I hurried across the room and drew the white curtains closed. My bag with clothes remained in the car, but for now, I wanted to dive into bed and forget the day.

Stripping down to my underwear, I switched off the main lights and climbed under the cold blankets. I curled in on myself and shut my eyes, pushing all my thoughts aside...everything but the heavy burden of loneliness remained. I nestled deeper into the pillow, breathing in the fresh clean smell with a calming hint of lavender.

Warm tears trickled down my cheeks, and I wiped them with my blanket, wondering how long before the ache in my chest for Alistair eased.

How long did it take to forget a fated mate? My heart pounded in my chest as I rolled over in bed.

I hated myself for feeling anything but hate for him.

I hated how much my body craved him.

I hated that it took me so long to finally escape him.

I hated myself.

Breathing heavily, I tucked myself tighter into a ball, unable to shake the feeling once again that I was indeed cursed.

~

I had to go somewhere. Now. Urgency pushed me to get moving. The only problem was that I couldn't remember where I was supposed to go. I'd forgotten.

Lofty pines surrounded me, thick with branches, the scent crisp on the air, while clouds gathered overhead, darkening the shadows. I rubbed the chill out of my arms, staring in every direction for anything familiar.

A sudden, piercing howl rang through the woods.

I twisted around on the spot fast, foliage cracking underfoot, the world seeming to darken so fast.

Where did I have to go? Remember, remember, remember.

The howl came again, and I flinched in my skin at the sharpness of the call.

Wolves.

A sudden glint of yellow flashed between two trees in the distance, like a reflection, except they were eyes.

Wolf eyes.

Fear tore through my chest.

I recoiled, stepping backward, never taking my gaze off the predator.

He watched me...waited. That's what they did before they attacked.

Just like Alistair. He had tested me, left the door open to our home, given me chances to escape. I only made that mistake once...that was all I needed to learn—he watched me. Broken ribs and a fractured hip were my lesson.

When the ear-piercing howl came again, my heart raced, and out of the shadows, a wolf the color of the blackest night lunged at me, teeth bared, death in his eyes.

~

I gasped and sat up in bed, covered in sweat, hair stuck to the sides of my face. My heart pounded in my chest. I gripped the blanket, drawing in rapid, shallow breaths, trying to recover from the nightmare. I glanced quickly around the room to make sure I was alone.

I'd been on the run for weeks and never had a dream

about Alistair until now. I just prayed it wasn't a premonition about this town.

Taking my time to let myself calm down, I finally shoved my legs out from under the blanket and got to my feet. Faint light glowed around the edges of the curtain, and I hurried across the room to where I could peer out from it.

Morning light drenched the woods in the distance, and down below lay the most glorious river, glinting beneath the sun like a chest of jewels. Across the bank, a green meadow spread outward, dotted in white flowers, along with at least a dozen cabin-like homes. Farther down the river, I spotted a bridge, made for cars to pass, and suddenly, the ghost town I'd stumbled into last night has been transformed into a picturesque scene so pretty, I couldn't have made it up. Perfect for anyone looking to get away. Maybe this was where all those earlier cars that had honked at me last night were rushing to.

Not that I could see any cars from up here.

No sounds came from outside my room either. It was strange how quiet this town appeared.

The fleeting thought came and went as I remembered I had a car to collect. I was already dreading seeing how badly it was damaged. I grabbed my clothes from the floor and headed into the shower.

Had luck actually been on my side for once in finding this place? I didn't want to push it.

I closed my eyes beneath the hot spray of water, starting to feel semi normal. Which was saying a lot, considering I've been on the road and spent many nights sleeping in my car. This was a luxury. I used the time to scrub my body with the little hotel soap and then lathered my hair with the hotel shampoo. It was apple-scented, and I smiled, almost forgetting how good a hot shower could feel.

Once I dried and pulled on my old clothes, I ran my fingers through my hair to chase away the tangles. I even used the small tube of toothpaste and the toothbrush supplied.

By the time I stepped out of my room, I felt brand new… if you didn't count the day old worn clothes I was wearing that were covered with dirt, sweat, and a little bit of blood from last night's adventure.

I headed downstairs where the hum of voices suddenly reached me, and instantly, my initial reaction was to pause, to back away. My body protested, and I retreated back up the steps.

I had to get my car somehow fixed and then leave. The more I kept moving across the country, the safer I'd be. Distance between Alistair and I was the answer.

Never stop in one place too long, Nelly had told me. *Keep going, and he won't track you down.*

Suddenly, Jim rounded the corner to come up the staircase, and I stiffened.

He paused, smiling, and the sunlight hitting the back of his head gave him a halo. For a moment, he reminded me of an angel. Maybe he was one, seeing as he offered me a sound sleep and food without so much as mentioning payment last night. Well not yet anyway… I still needed to work that part out.

"Morning. Carrie's just finished breakfast if you're hungry," he said chirpily, yet something danced behind his eyes, an uncertainty when he looked at me, just like last night, as though he knew something I didn't.

"Thank you. I'll be out of your hair soon." I followed him out into the main bar area. Again, the place remained empty. Jim led me to the far table right by the window where the sun lit up the spot like a beacon.

"I'll bring out the meal. Coffee, tea, or juice?"

"Coffee would be wonderful." I watched him head back quickly, noting he had a slight limp, and all I could think was that maybe I'd been too trusting, that I should have snuck out earlier, except then what? My car was still half attached to a tree.

I sighed.

Barely had I finished the thought when Jim reemerged carrying a black tray. He set it in front of me. Eggs, bacon, sausage. A bowl of fruit and yogurt. Toast and butter. My stomach betrayed me and growled. I hadn't eaten like this since I'd left.

"Carrie wasn't sure what you'd like. It's been a while since she had guests using our lodging."

I blinked up at him, my eyes pricking because so few people had been this kind to me before...well, not without wanting something in return. Which made me worry he'd expect something too.

"Well, dig in," he insisted.

"Thank you." I buttered the toast and started eating. Jim took a seat across from me as an older woman emerged from the kitchen who I assumed was his wife.

A slightly fuller woman around the waist, she dressed in a wraparound dress the color of the meadow outside that framed her curves perfectly. She had short hair and large, round, green eyes, and I immediately felt comfortable with her.

"Hello, dear, I'm Carrie." She came right over and gave me a half hug. A faint clementine scent overwhelmed me, and I held back the need to sneeze from the strong citrus perfume she wore.

"Jim tells me you're from out of town." She took a seat

next to her husband and rested her hands over her stomach, smiling. "Will you be staying with us for a bit then?"

I swallowed the mouthful of scrambled eggs.

"It all depends on my car—"

"The boys at our local mechanic towed it into town this morning," Jim explained.

"They did?" I almost choked on my food.

He nodded.

"Sure did. Well, after Jim here told them to get off their lazy asses and bring it in." Carrie smiled at me... She reminded me in part of my mother. The tenderness, the care in her eyes, the softness in her words...but that didn't make her safe, now did it?

"Where is it?" I lowered my fork.

"At the end of the main road, you can't miss the sign. Dentworks. They've probably already started working on it."

"Oh." The sound fell past my lips.

"Is something wrong?" Carrie asked.

"It's just that..." I licked my lips. "I don't really have enough money to pay for the car. Or for your generosity." Lowering my gaze, my cheeks burned with embarrassment that I said nothing of the kind to Jim last night. I had twenty dollars to my name, and that wasn't going to get me far.

"Are you in danger?" Carrie asked quietly and reached over the table, laying a hand on my arm. The tenderness brought tears to my eyes, a problem I'd had since I arrived here, but I blinked them away.

I looked over to the door, thinking it might be easier just to leave. I didn't want to talk about myself and definitely not with Jim and Carrie. Humans wouldn't understand the barbaric ways of wolf hierarchy, how females were objects to be owned, how I doubted Alistair would ever stop searching for me and that I had to keep running.

Carrie met my eyes, waiting for my response, a look of patience passing through her green gaze.

"I left home really fast." I peered over at them, but they didn't pepper me with questions. They just looked at me with sympathy. Something I didn't want, but I appreciated that over constant judgement. In all honesty, I wasn't sure what to do with such a reaction. I'd spent the last few years doing nothing but following rules and falling short, so this... this was refreshing.

"Your stay last night plus your meals are on the house. But I'm not sure if they will fix your car for free, unfortunately," Jim added.

A rush of emotion hit me again with his words. The concept of kindness was foreign to me, and I almost didn't know what to do with it. I cleared my throat, pushing away the pesky tears once again.

"What you've done is more than I expected. I'll find a way to pay you back somehow."

They simply smiled warmly in response. I tried to smile back, but it felt wrong on my lips. I hadn't smiled much in the past few years.

"I'm Rune by the way."

The door opened suddenly to the inn, and I jerked my head up at the screeching hinges of the door.

A young man, maybe eighteen or nineteen, marched inside, stomping across the floor and moving to stand behind the counter. His short black hair sat messily, shaved short at the sides. Rips streaked across the knees of his jeans, and his tee was so short that it revealed his midriff. He proceeded to pour himself a drink from what looked like a bottle of vodka, then drank the shot in one go before pouring another.

"Well, that's my call then." Jim sighed and got to his feet, then marched over to the man. "What happened, Daniel?" He pried the bottle from his hand.

"She kicked me out of the house, that's what's wrong. She kicked me out after she found the blood," he blasted, though Jim grabbed him by the elbow and dragged him into the kitchen and out of earshot hastily.

Blood?

"Listen, Rune," Carrie murmured, catching my attention. "If you need money, the local diner is looking for some help. Shouldn't take too long to save up enough to pay for the car fixes."

My mouth practically fell open. "Oh no, I can't stay here that long." I sank into the seat, realizing alternate options weren't exactly falling at my feet either. Then I backtracked, remembering how isolated this town was, how not many tourists stayed at the inn, and well, maybe staying a week or so here wouldn't be such a bad thing. Getting a small job meant making some much needed money. Then I could leave.

"Maybe you're right," I finally answered. "I can also pay you if I can keep staying here."

"Of course. Now, I better go join the other two before all hell breaks loose." She laughed, and I couldn't tell if that was a nervous reaction or a joke.

I finished my breakfast and stood up. The three of them stayed in the kitchen, and when their voices kept rising, I made a quick exit outside.

The thought of remaining in town didn't make it easier to breathe calmly when everything made me jump and I kept imagining Alistair stepping out from around a corner.

I blinked against the brightness outside and glanced out to the river and beyond it to the other side. An older woman stood in her doorway, staring my way like she'd seen a ghost, while a man was strolling towards the wood's edge that lay fifty yards beyond the cabins. I guessed people did live here after all.

I drew my gaze from the woman, my skin crawling from the attention, and quickly traveled around the inn.

I emerged onto a main road, which seemed to curve toward the river in the distance. Store fronts of all kinds lined the cobblestone sidewalk. The place held an old fairy-tale feel to it. Old thatched buildings with huge windows displaying goods from bread to clothes to a local grocer left me feeling like I'd stepped back in time to a historic town long forgotten. The river lay to my left, while on the right, goliath mountains rose in the background, the tops painted in snow.

I was walking through a postcard of a small town in the Alpine Mountains...that was the best way to describe this town.

With no one around, I assumed it was still too early in the morning, which was fine by me. I preferred not to be stared at like an animal in a zoo. I tucked my chin low and strolled down the road. I noted there were no cars on the street, and I wondered if not many people drove here.

Perhaps my assumption that tourists came here had been wrong. Though that surprised me with how beautiful and peaceful the place seemed.

I sauntered past a hair salon with a red-haired woman inside sweeping the floor, and I touched my hair absent-mindedly as I looked at my reflection in the glass of her salon. When was the last time I'd even done anything to my hair?

I grew up under lock and key, Alistair or one of his assholes came with me everywhere, and when you're being

watched, knowing that any wrong move came with reper-
cussions, you ended up hating outings.

Breathing deeply, I reminded myself I'd escaped and I
would do anything in my power to keep it that way.

Following the curve in the road, I noticed a young
couple strolling in my direction. They weren't holding
hands, but the proximity with which they walked said it all.
The woman was beautiful. She had liquid black hair that
cascaded over her shoulders, and she kept glancing up at
the man like nothing in the world compared.

Something in my chest stung to see such devotion, and
jealousy pierced through me that I'd never experience such
admiration directed towards me. That was how Alistair
should have looked at me. That was how I'd looked at him.

I glanced over to the man who towered over her, and my
steps faltered. He was stunning. The most stunning man I'd
ever seen.

He had hair as dark as hers. It was cut longer at the top
and shorter at the edges and back. My gaze danced over his
strong jawline with a shadow of growth, his thick
eyebrows...those full lips.

My insides tightened. That earlier sting now crashed
into me like a tremendous lightning storm striking. The two
of them looked perfect together. How were there people like
me in a world that also held them?

I continued to drink him in. Broad shoulders, a solid
body trimming down to a narrow waist, and trunk-like
thighs in deep blue Levis...the man was built and intimidating. And not someone I'd ever seen in real life... Men who
looked like him were fictional and in magazines.

He turned to face me, and I suddenly lost my breath. I
forgot my own name.

His deep, captivating green eyes hardened toward me. I shouldn't have been so caught in his gaze, but something about them stunned me at how easily they captured my attention.

No one had done this to me before.

No one ever.

No. One. Not even—

Who the heck was he?

His upper lip curled as if seeing me was anything but pleasant. They passed me, not moving out of the way, but forcing me to basically step off the sidewalk and onto the road.

The beautiful woman had eyes only for him, while he threw me a filthy glare and growled at me.

What the fuck?

I froze on the spot and turned to watch them vanish into one of the stores. Did that just happen?

Had he really just growled at me?

What an asshole.

Everything about his reaction told me he wasn't a fan of anyone new in his precious town. Why else would someone behave that way to a stranger? Well, unless he was completely crazy, which might be true.

And now I was berating myself for thinking for a second he was this spectacular Adonis.

I gritted my teeth, knowing I couldn't deny the thought, but that only made me more furious. I bet he was so used to women fawning over him, he could treat them like crap. The gorgeous ones were always assholes, didn't I know that?

I took a deep breath, wondering why I was getting so worked up over a pretty faced stranger. I probably wouldn't even see him again.

My breaths came faster, and I walked quickly in the

opposite direction from them, determined to put them out of my mind.

When a big sign across the road came into view, Dentworks, it only took seconds for my current state of mind to shift. If I was lucky, the car would be an easy fix, maybe they'd be kind and not charge me, and then I could be on my way.

I checked the road and crossed it quickly toward the automobile garage that lay open.

That was when I spotted my blue sedan glistening under the sunlight, but the closer I got, the more I saw the gravity of the damage done. The front of the car was completely crushed in from where I'd slammed into the tree. I cringed at how bad the wreckage was compared to what I remembered. But it had been dark. Now when I stared at the warped and twisted metal, my heart sunk. There was no way the car was drivable in this state.

Fuck!

I heard a crunch of feet on concrete behind me.

"Is it your car?" a voice asked me, and I turned to face a man in oil stained coveralls. Short hair, slightly curly, he stood with hands in his pockets nonchalantly. I was having trouble focusing on him with my wreck of a car sitting there. How long would I have to work at the diner to pay this off? And that was if I even got the job.

I was trapped here until I sorted out my car.

"Miss?"

I glanced back up at the guy, realizing I had completely forgotten to respond. "Y-yes, this is my car. How much is it going to cost to fix it?"

I chewed on my lower lip, praying the news wasn't as severe as the damage on the car.

"Sorry, ma'am, but we only just hauled it here, so maybe

come back later when the bossman is in to see when he can fit it in."

I licked my suddenly dry lips. "But if you had to take a guess. How much would such a fix cost?"

He shrugged and ran a hand over his mouth, staring at the mess behind me. "It's impossible to tell until we see the internal damage to the motor, but it'll probably run into the thousands."

"Thousands?" My knees weakened. I might as well buy a second-hand car for that cost.

"Like I said, we won't know until we pull it apart." He started strolling back into the garage, while I was left looking at the chaotic mess I'd made of my car.

I wanted to cry so badly. For weeks, I'd been careful, then a damn animal darting across the road ruined everything.

I took in deep inhales to calm myself, but all I managed was to drown on the oxygen.

Then I recalled my bag was still in the car, so I approached the back door and pulled it open. It sat there waiting for me. I reached in and grabbed it, along with my half-eaten Doritos bag and bottle of water.

I shot a glare at my car for putting me in this spot. Which was ridiculous since it was my fault. With a huff, I walked down the driveway, figuring this was as good a time as any to find the diner and apply for a job. I returned to the inn to put on something more presentable, not that I had many options.

Fifteen minutes later, I stood in front of Moonstruck Diner, an older building with a wide, wraparound window that guided me to the entrance door at the side. It didn't look busy.

A bell rang when I pushed open the door and stepped

inside. Booths lined the window, while smaller black and white chairs and tables peppered the main area. The ordering bar was located to the far right with the kitchen tucked behind the counter with a swinging door and a service window giving me a view of a man with his back to me. Farther in the back was a small bar with stools and what looked like a small stage for a band.

Wooden floorboards, bright globe light fixtures hung over the booths, and smaller ones lit up the rest of the room. The place looked loved and heavily used.

The smell of eggs and toast permeated the air, and I glanced past the only patron in the room glancing my way. My attention swept toward the kitchen section, where a man stepped out and immediately lifted his gaze to meet mine.

My heart beat tremendously fast. I wiped my sweaty palms down my black skirt, and I prayed he didn't notice the wrinkles in my white shirt. The room at the inn had no iron I could find.

Before I could find my confidence, the man approached me with a wide smile and long strides. He wore jeans and a black button-up shirt with the word 'Moonstruck' over his heart and a half rising moon over the words. The badge above the logo on his shirt revealed his name. Marcus.

"Table for one?" he asked. "And looks like it's your lucky day. You can pick your table. It's not often we get out of town visitors."

This really must be a small town if he could take one look at me and know I was from out of town. Thinking on it, it had been that way with everyone.

He paused in front of me, standing much taller than I was, his dark russet hair messy around his angular face. The wheels behind his brown eyes were spinning. No denying, the man was extremely easy on the eyes, and there was a commanding feel about the way he carried himself. I recognized strength and leadership in this man. It was the small things, the way he stood, holding my stare, every word calculated.

Much like Alistair, except this man was hopefully nothing like my fated mate. Alistair had kept me his prisoner for so long where I had no say, no identity, no strength to stand up for myself. He stripped me bare of everything, making me so scared that I behaved as he'd expected.

When I looked at Marcus, I didn't see cruelty, just uncertainty and hesitation.

I could work with that.

"Actually, I'm here to apply for the waitress position." Sweat dripped down my back, and I hated how nervous I felt. "My name's Rune." I stuck my hand out to shake his, unsure if that was the right thing to do in this situation.

He didn't leave me hanging for long and shook my hand. His grip was strong, his touch hot.

Hold it together and keep smiling.

But when he didn't respond, anxiety beat into me that I'd come too late and the position was filled.

"I'm a hard worker and a quick learner, plus I can start today if you need me..." The words rushed out desperately, and I fidgeted awkwardly in place.

The truth was I'd never had a job. But I could learn. I tried out a smile again, inwardly wincing at how awkward I was sure it looked.

He sighed. "We're still discussing with the team if we need an extra helping hand, so no news on it yet."

"Marcus, who are you kidding?" the man at the booth by the window called out. "This place is a shit show right now. We need help."

I wanted to hug the stranger for stepping in.

Marcus threw a glare at the man, so I seized the opportunity.

"Please. Try me out for a week or two and let me show you my worth."

He ran a hand through his hair. "How about you come back in a few days, and I'll have a talk with the owner."

His words gutted me, and my attempt to appear professional and in control flew out the window.

As he turned away from me, I pleaded, "Please, I really need this job. I've run out of options. I'll do anything, even scrub the toilets if that's what you need."

I loathed listening to myself, but reality was a brutal bastard. With only twenty dollars in my purse, I had no car or way of getting out of his town. If I tried to leave here right now, I would have no roof over my head, and where would I even go? I was in the middle of nowhere with wolves in the woods.

I trembled at the thought.

The bell from the front door opened, and a party of three older men entered, chatting, not even paying us attention as they made their way to the farthest booth.

"You seem really nice, Rune, but—"

"P-please." I stepped closer and lowered my voice. "I'll be honest with you, Marcus. My car is ruined, and I don't have money. If I don't find a way to pay for the repairs, I'm homeless and stuck here. I'm sorry, I hate saying this or putting you on the spot. Carrie from the inn mentioned you had a position."

I tried to think about other options I had. There wouldn't be a lot of open jobs in a small town like this. I could ask Jim if he had a job to help in the bar, but he probably would have said something if that was an option. There were a number of other stores in town, and I guessed I could try every one of them. My heart started to race at the prospect.

Marcus swallowed loudly, his lips pursed. Then he released a long exhale, and I knew I'd broken him down. "You start the day after tomorrow. Be here at six p.m. sharp. We won't have time for a lot of training, so you'll have to show us how quickly you can pick things up."

My eyes widened. "Oh my goodness, I can't thank you enough. This means everything to me."

He nodded curtly. "I'm giving you a chance. Don't let me down."

"I promise." I nodded.

"Good. See you soon, Rune." He moved toward the newcomers, and that was my cue to leave.

To say my chest was bursting with excitement was an understatement.

I'd just gotten a job. I couldn't believe it. I wanted to scream in excitement that for the first time in so long, something went right.

Making my way back to the inn, I practically skipped along the sidewalk, which wasn't like me.

But I had a job!

My cheeks hurt from smiling so much.

Farther ahead, more people were walking around the main road and into stores, the town finally coming to life with activity. Every person I passed had a weird reaction when they saw me though. A flare of anxiety darted through me. People were kind of weird in this town. I couldn't work out what it was, but things felt...off center.

Despite my good news, I tried to piece together the strangeness of today. Blood mentioned by the young guy in the inn. The way people watched me like they'd never seen an outsider in their town. Then there was that angry hot guy with his girlfriend who growled at me. A fluttery feeling hit my stomach at the thought of him, followed by a rush of anger.

I had a lot of experience in the danger of good-looking men. I'd be staying as far away from him as possible.

But as long as I didn't cross paths with him again and I could get used to strange looks, staying in town might just be bearable.

3

RUNE

I laid in bed the next morning, listening to the sounds of the river floating through the open window. I was beginning to be convinced that listening to running water should be a form of therapy. Or maybe it was? I'd have to look into that.

I sighed and closed my eyes, relaxing into the soft sheets. I wasn't used to this...peace. Was that what this feeling was? I tried to remember the last time I'd felt something like this.

Was it never?

My hands shook as I sprinkled the powder that Nelly gave me in the drinks. If anyone ever knew she had helped me, she'd be killed. But I couldn't do it. Not one more day. I couldn't do it.

I would rather die.

Which would also happen if I stayed here any longer.

I stirred the powder into the brandy Alistair had barked at me to get for him and his friends.

Nelly had promised me that this stuff was tasteless. But I was the unluckiest person on earth, so all I could hope was that she was right.

"Rune, you piece of trash, get your ass in here." Alistair's

comments were followed by the raucous laughter of him and his betas, all as high up on the asshole scale as he was.

I tried to still the shaking of my hands as I carried the tray of drinks into the living room where the men were sprawled out smoking cigars. A smoky haze filled the room, and I choked on a cough. The entire mansion would smell like the skunky cigars for the rest of the week. That, and sex. I'm sure they were expecting their usual prostitutes to show up tonight too. Good thing Nelly had made sure that order was cancelled.

"What are you waiting for?" Alistair growled out. I didn't paste a fake smile on my face, that would be too suspicious.

I began to hand out the drinks. Desmond, the beta of the pack that I hated the most, reached out a claw when I began to hand him his. The jerk cackled loudly when I flinched back. He took every opportunity to rub in the fact that I would never be able to shift. I hated him.

I hated them all.

I finished handing out the drinks and went to wait in the corner of the room where I usually would be spending the rest of the night, waiting for Alistair to give me orders.

Tonight was going to be different though.

As the seven men sipped on their drinks and in general acted like the enormous douchebags that they were, my mind went crazy with all the possible things that could go wrong.

What if they didn't all fall asleep? What if one of them was immune? What if one of them was just pretending to drink and he never ingested the powder?

My worries went on and on. There was so much at stake.

An hour later, they were all fast asleep in various places around the room. The powder had hit all of them within a few seconds span of each other, so no one had time to warn anyone else that something was wrong.

It was time.

Taking a deep breath, I darted from my corner of the room and went over to Alistair, where he had fallen asleep with his head on one of his beta's shoulders, a position that Alistair would find incredibly embarrassing normally.

I picked up his arm and then heaved his body against my shoulder, almost crumbling under the weight. My broken rib on my left side screamed with the effort. This wasn't going to work. Alistair had given me that particular injury a few days ago when I'd accidently dropped a plate in the kitchen as I was putting dishes away from dinner. It had been a rather nasty beating because he'd also accused me of staring a little too long at the visitor we had from the Redmond Pack that night. Of course, since my wolf had never been released, I had no shifter powers to help me heal, so I would have to deal with the pain for weeks just like a normal human.

Internally freaking out that I hadn't thought everything through as much as I should have, I grabbed a blanket from the couch and dropped Alistair on it, enjoying the sound of his head cracking against the tile floor a little too much.

I grabbed two of the blanket ends and began to drag Alistair across the floor to the hallway where his office was. Sweat dripped down my forehead from the amount of effort it took to drag a six foot four, two hundred and thirty-five pound man across a room. I was five foot nine, tall for a woman, but no match for Alistair's size.

I had to take breaks every couple of steps. The pain in my ribs was better than it had been when I was trying to lean him against me, but pulling on the blanket was still excruciating.

I just prayed that the powder would actually last the eight to ten hours that Nelly had suggested because this seemed to be taking forever.

I made it to the hallway and took another break. Sweat dripped down on the tiled floor below me. My breath came out in tortured gasps. Taking another deep breath, I pulled on the blanket, groaning with the effort, and this time, finally made it into Alistair's office...where his safe was held.

That safe was going to be my ticket out of here. Alistair's presence was required because the safe needed his thumbprint and a retina scan in order to open. I'd been tempted to chop them off and save myself the effort of dragging Alistair into the room, but I'd figured he'd be mad enough once he woke up. I didn't need to add the rage he'd experience if he had to grow back an eyeball and a hand at the same time.

I got him over to the safe and then realized I was an idiot.

The safe was behind the typical picture frame. The picture frame was bolted to the wall at the top and had to be held to the side when opening the safe. If I had my shifter powers, I'd be able to hold up Alistair and the picture frame with ease. But since I didn't, I didn't see how it was possible to do it.

I was actually going to have to cut his hand and eyeball off.

Holy shit.

There was no time for me to come up with a different plan. My hands trembled as I grabbed from the wall one of the long swords Alistair had decorated the room with. It was supposed to belong to some ancient conqueror of China... Was it the Huns? The sword was heavy in my arms, and I worried for a second, imagining having to hack my way through Alistair's wrist instead of the clean swipes I always saw other members of the pack accomplish.

Giving myself an internal pep talk, I brought the sword up as high as I could manage and then sliced it down on Alistair's wrist.

Blood spewed everywhere, but the cut went clean through. Evidently, Alistair had made sure the sword stayed very sharp. That attention to detail, along with the money I knew was in the safe, were really Alistair's only redeeming qualities I could think of in the moment.

I didn't feel bad about slicing his wrist off at all.

It was a testament to how strong the powder was that Alistair didn't move at all during any of this. He laid there peacefully, even as blood poured out of the wound.

The next part was going to be the really bad part though. I was just going to have to stop myself from puking, or at least aim it over Alistair's body.

I needed a small knife. I started out of the room, sliding a little bit in the blood that coated the previously pristine white floor. I ran to the kitchen and got a small steak knife and then made my way back, checking the living room as I went to make sure it was still as quiet as I'd left it.

Everyone was still sleeping peacefully.

I made it back to the office. "Ok, you can do this," I coached myself as I lifted Alistair's right eyelid. His eye stared at me blankly.

I cut that son of a bitch's eye out then, and I managed to only puke once...right on his face.

I set the disgusting eyeball and Alistair's right hand on the desk beside the wall and then lifted the painting to the side.

Why did it have to be so heavy?

The safe looked like something from a Bond movie but I'd seen Alistair get into it enough to know how it worked. I pressed a few buttons and then grabbed Alistair's hand and pressed it to the scanner, signing in relief when it accepted his print. I belatedly realized that I could have just chopped his thumb off, but considering everything Alistair had done to me and taken from me, he could deal with more pain.

Next up was the eyeball. I held down the urge to retch once again as I touched it and held it up to the scanner, hoping I hadn't damaged the retina at all while I was tearing the eyeball out.

When it worked and the safe door popped open, I almost cried.

Alistair had stacks of cash in the safe, and I quickly grabbed five of the stacks, carefully avoiding the ones with a green dot on the band that held the cash together. Those had a tracker on them. Alistair was suspicious and thought everyone had an eye on his cash. He would periodically put trackers on his expensive items. This included his collection of jewels, artwork, antiques, weaponry...and his cash.

I'd picked today because he'd just gotten this cash this morning from whatever drug sale he'd recently completed, and Nelly had conveniently not gotten to placing the trackers yet.

She was an angel.

And Alistair was going to make her pay for that.

Shaking that dark thought off, I took the money and then ran to my bedroom to grab the bag I'd stashed in the back of the closet under a pile of dirty clothes. Throwing the money in there, I readied myself to leave. There was a bus leaving in thirty minutes that would take me to a town an hour away from here where Nelly said there was a car salesman that was well-versed in quiet, under the table transactions.

I was almost there.

As I rushed to leave, my footsteps faltered outside the office where my mate still lay sleeping.

I couldn't resist taking one last look at him.

I stood over his body, just staring at him. My brain raged for me to kill him, to take the sword and hack off his head. I knew Alistair kept silver bullets in the safe, just in case a rogue pack of shifters ever attacked. It was all right there, the keys to end it all.

But I couldn't do it.

Alistair was beautiful, even now dressed in blood and the last few years of pain, agony, and disappointment. His hair was matted with blood and puke currently, but it was usually a perfect shade of sable brown flecked with streaks of gold. He had a gaping hole where his eye had been, but the grisly sight couldn't make me forget how brilliant of a green they normally were. I'd been enamored with them...with him from the start.

I'd loved him. I'd thought he was my hero.

And even though the truth of him was forever etched in my soul, I couldn't do it. I couldn't kill him.

I may have been a coward for walking away and leaving him there.

But it would be like killing myself to take his life right now.

And I was already dead enough inside.

I tore myself away from the memory and sat up in bed, my whole body trembling. Pain ripped through me as I tried to push the image of Alistair away. It wasn't getting easier. Did he feel this too? Like he was a half a person? Or was his heart already so destroyed that the agony was nothing to him?

I put my face in my hands and tried not to weep with frustration.

After Alistair had revealed himself, I'd spent a lot of time raging at the universe for how unfair it was that this was my fate. But eventually, I'd come to accept I wasn't the master of my universe. The moon goddess was in charge, and for some reason, she had decided this path for me.

It helped, telling myself that I wasn't in control.

So I was a little out of sorts sitting here in my bed, realizing that for the first time in a very long time...I did have some control of my destiny.

I didn't know what I thought about that.

Determined to get as much done as possible today since I would be starting work later on, I dragged myself out of bed and got dressed in a pair of cut-off shorts and an artfully ripped T-shirt I'd found in the bargain bin at Target before my money had been stolen. It read 'Savage'...which had seemed funny to me at the time, considering I'd just cut a man's eyeball out, but I wasn't sure how appropriate it was for a place like this.

It was all I had though until I found a laundromat and a second-hand store...and got some money. So it would have to do.

Carrie was working the front desk when I walked into the lobby. She waved me over before I could slip out. Reaching under the counter, she pulled out a selection of pastries and donuts and a paper cup filled with coffee. "You need to eat something, young lady. I noticed you eyeing the chocolate donuts yesterday, so I hid some away for you today."

My heart did that thing again...where it felt. Chocolate donuts on lazy Sunday mornings had been my mom's and my thing. Although I'd tried to get rid of anything that reminded me of her, my love for chocolate donuts hadn't been easily eradicated.

"Thank you," I said, doing that awkward throat clearing thing which was fast becoming a necessity in this place.

I stuffed the donut in my mouth, hoping the chewing would spare me from chatting.

Don't get me wrong, I wanted to be the kind of person that could chat for hours with a sweetheart like Carrie. I just didn't possess those skills anymore.

After I'd managed to inhale the donut and take a few swallows of the coffee...which somehow tasted better than any coffee I'd ever had before, I waved goodbye and hurried out onto the sidewalk. I took a deep breath of air, enjoying the breeze on my face. Out here in the sunshine, I could almost believe good things were possible.

Almost.

I was only huffing slightly by the time I made it to Dentworks. Exercise was definitely in order if I actually stayed here for any length of time. Next time I had to run for my life, it would be nice to do it without the risk of fainting from hyperventilating too hard.

I looked around for the man from the day before, but he was nowhere to be found. The garage opening where my car had been yesterday was closed, so I followed the sound of tools clanging and hitting metal from nearby until I found three huge stations, one with two cars deep...and the other filled with motorcycles. A crew of workers were working on them while they laughed and teased each other.

I shifted uncomfortably at the sight of so many men all together. There were at least ten of them. A particularly loud laugh had me backing up a few steps and debating whether I should come back later.

Flashbacks cycled through my brain of the games Alistair and his betas used to play with me...the way they tortured me for fun.

"What do you want?" an exasperated voice barked. "The hair salon's down the street."

My insides hackled at his tone. I looked to the side and saw an older man, maybe in his early sixties. He stared at me under shaggy, grizzled eyebrows, his brown eyes full of disdain and annoyance. His brown hair was frizzy and liberally streaked with grey, and it was badly in need of a trim. He was wearing grease streaked grey overalls over a stained white tee that had seen better days. The man would have been intimidating enough with his gaze alone, but the fact that he was a giant...at least six foot five or six, had me shaking in my boots.

"My car," I squeaked, unable to look him in the eyes. I had no idea where my wolf sat on the whole dominant-submissive spectrum since I'd obviously never met her, but

Alistair had instilled in me the notion that you didn't look a man in the eye.

It was a habit I was trying to break.

He looked around. "Is your car invisible?"

I looked at him, puzzled.

"I don't see a car," he said as if I was slow, gesturing around me.

I laughed nervously, spotting it in one of the garages behind him and gesturing to it. "It's that one."

"That piece of shit? That's not going anywhere any time soon. You make a habit of running into trees?"

I scoffed, caught between wanting to defend myself and wanting to cower from the anger that was inexplicably laced through this guy's body. Was there something in the water here that had these random strangers biting my head off, or was it just me?

The snarl of a motorcycle distracted me from the retort that was on the tip of my tongue. The man looked behind me at whoever was driving up and straightened his shoulders, puffing his chest out as if he needed to impress the newcomer.

I turned around as the engine shut off...and my jaw dropped.

There was a golden god in front of me looking like he'd just dropped down from the heavens. Hazel eyes flecked with gold were framed by dark long lashes that any woman would be envious of. But there was nothing feminine about this guy. His hair itself was like spun gold, each thread falling effortlessly to frame his tanned face. He was sitting on his bike, loosely holding onto the handlebars. I found myself staring at his fingers and wondering how I could find even those hot. They were long but strong looking, his fingernails pink and smooth, with half-moons near the cuticles. My eyes wandered up his arm next, to the hint of a strong forearm that disappeared into the sleeve of his leather jacket, because of course the hot guy had to be wearing a leather jacket on top of everything else. I watched his hand as it moved up to rub his chin as he stared at me curiously. His nose was straight and aquiline, his lips were perfectly formed and parted slightly.

I was having trouble not swooning.

An image of the dark-haired asshole with his girlfriend from the day before danced across my brain. This guy could even rival him in looks, even though they were complete opposites. My body would probably burst into flames if I ever got into the same room as the both of them.

My vagina was praying for it to happen.

"Hey, sweetheart," he drawled, and I found that my panties were suddenly feeling a bit damp. I shifted nervously in place again. I felt pinned in place by his intense gaze. It was dancing all over me like he couldn't decide what he wanted to look at. His hand moved from his chin to his bottom lip, and all I could think about was what his lips would taste like.

I shook my head, becoming aware again of the grumpy old guy still standing behind me. I could feel his irritation growing the longer I stood there, so I lamely waved at the hot Adonis before turning back around to deal with my car problem.

"When you say 'not any time soon,' how long exactly is that?" I asked, my gaze flicking to my car, which somehow looked even worse today.

The grump rolled his eyes once again and opened his mouth, I'm sure to deliver another stinging remark about my driving abilities.

"You giving this pretty girl a hard time, North?" the

stranger asked, his smooth voice sending delicious shivers down my spine. Something stirred inside of me, and I froze in place, not recognizing the feeling.

Rude guy, aka North apparently, growled at the guy's question. The sound reverberated through me, familiar and unfamiliar at the same time. Did normal humans growl like that? He almost sounded wolf-like. I laughed at the thought, thinking that was preposterous.

I heard movement behind me, and I shuffled to the side so that I could see both of the men at the same time. One thing you're taught as a wolf shifter, even a latent one like me, was that you watched your flank. These were definitely two men that you watched out for.

Golden god slid off his black Harley with ease. His shirt slid up with his movement, showcasing a sliver of hard muscle, the same golden shade as the rest of him. Ugh, he was beautiful.

"North?" the man questioned, standing up to his full height which was almost as tall as North was. But there was something in his voice, a thread of authority that was missing in North's. It made me want to offer my neck to him in submission...

What the hell? That was a strange thought. That funny feeling happened again, like something was coming to life in my chest. I rubbed my chest absentmindedly as I continued to stare at the two of them.

There was a tick in North's cheek as he held the gaze of the other man. A low growl erupted from the golden guy's throat, and I watched, entranced, as he lowered his gaze.

I was imagining this, right? Maybe this was how the real world worked for everyone—alpha males struggling for dominance.

I shook my crazy thoughts away. Alistair had been fanatical about the threat of other packs. Their location and size had been meticulously kept track of. One of the reasons I was driving in this part of the country in the first place was because there were no packs around here. My brain was just imagining things, trying to find the familiar in the unfamiliar.

Right?

"I was in the process of helping her when you interrupted, Daxon," North finally retorted in a gravelly voice. Daxon... I liked that name. It was unique and beautiful. Just like him.

I couldn't help but snort, and both of them looked at me. One gaze filled with amusement, the other filled with disgust. He had totally been "helping me." Insert eye roll.

"Your ride acting up again?" North asked, his gaze practically caressing Daxon's ride. I didn't blame him for the way he looked like he wanted to make babies with Daxon's Harley. Even I thought the bike was gorgeous. And I knew nothing about motorcycles.

"Something's wrong with the clutch again," Daxon said on a sigh, glancing down at the bike with frustration.

"Johnson," North barked, and a tattooed beast of a man strolled out of the garage, wiping his grease covered hands on a dirty rag. He gave me a wink as he walked up to us, his gaze sauntering up my body and making me blush with the clear connotation he was giving me.

A low growl filled the air, and I glanced at Daxon, who was glaring at Johnson like he'd punched his grandma. Johnson immediately stopped looking at me and took a step back nervously.

Interesting.

"Take a look at Daxon's clutch. Make sure it's fixed this time," North snapped exasperatedly.

This guy really was not a people person.

"Sure thing..." Johnson hesitated, his gaze twitching to me. "Daxon."

These people were kind of weird.

"It's going to be maybe two months to get it fixed, if we can get all the parts we need quickly. And that's if we open the hood and everything isn't destroyed," North announced, staring at my car as if it personally offended him. "I'll tell you right now that it's not worth fixing though. The thing's a piece of trash."

I ignored his last statement. "And how much do you think it's going to cost?" I asked, dread infused in my voice. The guy yesterday had said thousands, but maybe he'd been wrong.

"More money than it's worth," North drawled. "Around ten thousand, give or take a few a thousand."

"Ten thousand dollars?" I asked, feeling faint. I stumbled backwards, and a strong pair of hands suddenly steadied me. For a second, I leaned into their warmth before realizing it was Daxon holding me. How had he gotten behind me so fast?

Men were not allowed to touch me. Especially strange men. I darted forward as if his hands had burned me, ignoring the decidedly pleasant sensation I'd actually experienced at his touch.

When I turned around, a little ashamed at my reaction to normal human touch, Daxon was studying me intensely, a puzzled look on his face as he did so.

"It's going to take me some time to earn that kind of money," I admitted to North. "But I just got a job at the diner down the street. I'll be saving every penny."

North shook his head in disgust. "I'm not in the business of charity, lady. I'm not like the rest of these fools that can be distracted by a pretty face. Take your car and get the hell out of here," he snarled.

Despite the fact he'd just metaphorically kicked me in the gut, something inside me warmed at the insinuation that *I* was pretty. I hadn't felt pretty...not in years. Even coming from someone who had the jerk title firmly won...it kind of felt good.

I was pathetic.

"I'll spot her when it's ready," Daxon said casually, as if it was no big deal that he'd offered to help a complete stranger.

"Of course," North spit under his breath.

I stared at Daxon in shock...and suspicion. "I—Why would you do that? You don't even know me." Shaking my head at him, I turned my attention back to North. "This wouldn't be a charity case. You said I have a few months. If you could just work on it slowly while I save the money." I told him, determination leaking into my voice as I straightened my shoulders and tried to look fierce...or dependable. One of the two.

North stared at me for a long moment, something shifting behind his gaze. "I'll put it as a last priority. But if you don't have the full amount by the time it's done..." He growled loudly, shaking his head as he stormed away.

My bravado dropped as soon as he wasn't looking at me. I was going to have to sell plasma or something. There was no way I could earn that kind of money at the diner, not even if I turned out to be the most amazing waitress on earth. Something I seriously doubted I would be...

"Hey," Daxon said gently, touching my cheek softly, making me flinch once again.

"Please don't touch me," I whispered, frustration clogging my words.

He held up his hands. "We're a little bit friendly around here. It's just a habit. I won't do it again. Not unless you ask."

I tried to hide my swoon when he winked at me. Was he hitting on me?

"What's your name?" he asked, cocking his head and giving me a flirty grin. The guy could smile. My ovaries were working overtime just looking at him do it.

I hesitated before giving it to him. That feeling in my stomach was on overdrive as I stared at him.

"Rune," I finally answered.

"Rune," he said softly, as if he was savoring the taste of my name. The way he said it sent images of rumpled sheets, soft sighs, a heaviness between my thighs.

"You okay?" he questioned, cutting off the highly inappropriate and out of character daydream I was having standing there.

I blushed what I was sure was a thousand shades of red. "I have to go," I blurted, turning around and practically bolting away.

"We'll talk about the loan!" I yelled over my shoulder, well aware of his gaze all over my skin and the amused smile on his face that I desperately wanted to take a picture of.

The men in this town were going to be a hazard to my health. Just in a different way from how Alistair was.

Men, I thought disgustedly under my breath as I darted around the corner, finally out of his line of sight.

This town was turning out to be more than I'd bargained for.

~

J was itching to run. I'd been on the track team in middle school and high school, and it had been one of my favorite things to do. The rush of runner's high, the breeze floating past your face, the ability to forget your problems with every step. I'd loved everything about it. Alistair had quickly put a stop to it, deciding that it would bring too much temptation for me, but now that he wasn't around...

I laced up my sneakers. After I'd escaped, they had been the second thing I'd bought after my now defunct car. Tonight would be my first run, and I already could taste the inner Zen I was about to experience.

Waving at Carrie, who looked strangely worried as I slipped out the door, I set off down the sidewalk.

And immediately regretted every single bag of potato chips I'd consumed on my little road trip. As a latent wolf, I didn't have the metabolism I would have had if Alistair, my alpha, had released my wolf. It was a small thing compared to everything else, but I was definitely raging about it as I huffed and puffed down the sidewalk, looking more like a beached barracuda than the graceful gazelle I liked to think I'd once resembled.

It was still daylight outside, so I felt comfortable taking the road that led down to the river, and maybe the view would distract me from how hard I was breathing. I still couldn't get over the beauty of this place. I didn't know how they managed to stay so under the radar. I watched as a freaking bald eagle soared just a few feet away.

Magical.

After a measly twenty-minute run where every step felt far from the runner's high I'd once been familiar with, I finally had to stop and catch my breath. My heart was racing out of control, and I decided that tomorrow, I'd be asking Carrie for some egg whites and saying no to the chocolate donuts.

Except that donut had been so freaking good.

My musings about the pros and cons of Doritos and chocolate donuts were cut off by a low growl just off to my left. I froze, my heart racing even more as a sable colored wolf stepped into view out of the tree line that lined the river trail. It just stared at me for a moment before its lips curled back to expose pearl white fangs.

It only flashed its teeth for a second, but it was enough to give me a small heart attack. I stumbled backwards as it sat down on its haunches and cocked its head, staring at me a little too intelligently.

"Nice doggy," I whispered, continuing to back up while keeping eye contact the entire time.

It growled in response as if it could understand me. I was really wishing I had a wolf's sense of smell right about now, because I'd never seen a wild wolf act like this.

It gave one more growl and then abruptly swung around and trotted back into the underbrush and trees.

I ran as fast as I could back to the hotel without looking back. Looked like it was just going to be runs through town from now on.

This place had a wolf problem.

As I made it back to the hotel as the sun started to fade, I wasn't aware of the motorcycle parked in the dim lighting just down the street. And the man on that bike who watched me.

*J*n the shower, I'd managed to convince myself that I had no actual idea how wild wolves acted and I was just imagining things that weren't there. I refused to believe that my curse would extend to sending me straight to shifters after I'd vowed I would never be near one again.

The bar was actually full without a seat to spare when I ventured downstairs into the lobby. I decided to get food somewhere else. The weather was perfect outside, but the streets were quiet, just like the night I'd arrived. I strolled down the sidewalk, looking in the store windows as I passed. A door opened a few buildings down, bringing with it the sound of music and laughter. A couple staggered out the door, practically tearing each other's clothes off as they stumbled away. Intrigued, I walked closer and saw a sign for the Jaw Bone Pub. The place didn't look like much, but the smell coming out of it was incredible. Maybe I could venture in and grab a cup of soup or something from the grocery store.

The moment I stepped through the heavy wooden door, I was assaulted by a cacophony of sounds and smells that had my senses whirling. My insides were going haywire, like something was jumping around. I needed to find some Tums somewhere. The feeling wasn't unpleasant, but it had to be related to some stomach issues because it wasn't anything I'd experienced before.

The place wasn't that crowded. There were a few people at a long, polished wooden bar, and a few others scattered in tables around the large room. There was a dancefloor on the far side with a scuffed up black floor and an old-fashioned jukebox. And there were wolves.

Not literally.

But there were wolves engraved everywhere. On the chair backs, in the bar, in the beams on the ceiling. I glanced back at the door that had just closed behind me, not surprised at all to see a giant wolf engraved in it. There was even a gorgeous wooden wolf sculpture behind the bar designed to look like the wolf was emerging from the wall. The details were so perfect, I half expected for the sculpture to come alive at any moment and the wolf to spring the rest of the way into the room.

A brunette with skin the color of cinnamon was polishing glasses behind the bar. She watched me suspiciously as I walked to the bar and settled into one of the high-backed leather chairs. The woman was wearing a cut off shirt that barely covered her ample chest and low slung jeans. Her abdomen was tight and toned, and for a second, I contemplated asking for workout tips because she looked like she could throw down.

"Hi," I said politely. "Can I see a menu?"

She smacked a piece of gum loudly and then threw a faded, torn piece of paper without saying a word.

Oh goodie, another friendly town resident.

I gave a sigh of relief that the prices were really low and ordered a water, a bowl of soup, and a side of bread.

The bartender nodded and then disappeared for a moment before coming back and resuming polishing the glasses. I looked around the room and noticed most of the inhabitants seemed to be watching me either outright or out of the corner of their eye.

This was going to be a quick dinner.

"So...you guys sure seem to like your wolves here. Is it because of the wolves in the woods?" When I was nervous, I either couldn't talk or I had word vomit.

This was the latter.

The woman barked out a laugh and looked at me incredulously. When she saw I was serious, her laughter abruptly cut off. "You could say that," she finally said, her voice low and cool.

A guy and a girl a few seats down from me were still laughing at my comment, and I pursed my lips, determined to keep quiet.

No one tried to talk to me, and my food came out five minutes later, allowing me to focus on that instead of the awkward silence that had descended on the room the second I'd walked in.

I was just a few bites in of the delicious soup when suddenly, a rancid smell hit me. I set my spoon down, wrinkling my nose in disgust and looking around the room. The smell dissipated after a moment, and then I was struck by an intense aroma of body odor. It resembled cheese that had been left in the back of a broken refrigerator...for a month. It hit me just as a pudgy guy with sweat-stained pits passed behind me. Ugh. He desperately needed to be introduced to deodorant.

I noticed the bartender watching me closely again. "A lot of interesting smells," I told her, unable to shut myself up.

She just gave me a weird little smile, like she knew something I didn't.

"Can I get this to go?" I asked, my previously ferocious appetite a bit quelled with the overload of odors in the room. The longer I sat here, the more I was experiencing, and I was getting overwhelmed.

"Sure thing," she replied curtly before printing out my bill and throwing me a Styrofoam to-go container.

I made sure to leave a tip, even though her service had been far from good. Karma and all that.

"You'll get used to it," she told me cryptically as I stood to go.

I looked at her uncomprehending.

"The smells. You get used to it," she clarified before disappearing in the back.

Shaking my head at the weirdness of everyone here, I grabbed my food and wandered back to the inn.

The sounds of wolves howling in the distance followed me all the way back.

I spent most of the next day worrying and thinking about my first shift at the diner. I was ready an hour early and spent most of that hour pacing around my room.

Finally, it was time.

The door to Moonstruck Diner swung open right as I reached for it, and I quickly stepped back, barely avoiding being smacked in the face as three men walked out. The men were deep in laughter, not paying me any attention.

A fact I was glad for, in all honesty.

I caught the door before it shut and slipped inside to my new place of work. My stomach churned with nerves as a heavy wave of smells hit me, mostly the various foods being cooked and the heavy bitter scent of beer. Thankfully, it wasn't a horrible smell like it had been the previous night at the bar.

It couldn't be that hard to be a waitress, right? I'd even practiced smiling last night because I thought that would help with tips, something I was doubting based on how bad I still was at it.

I couldn't afford to make a single mistake. I had to save at least ten thousand dollars. I almost fainted thinking of that amount again. My plan was simple. Work however long it took to pay off the car, then I would high-tail it out of this weird-ass town.

Looking down at myself, I wore the closest thing I had to waitress attire. A black, tight skirt that fell just above my knees and a matching shirt, trying to mimic Marcus' uniform as closely as possible.

Unlike the previous time I'd been in, the diner was busy. Scratch that...busy was too tame a word. Chaotic better suited the place. Nearly every seat was filled. The song, "Back to Black" by Amy Winehouse played overhead, and one poor waitress was rushing off her feet, delivering meals, taking orders, darting from one table to the next.

A sharp bell rang from the kitchen window in the back corner where I watched the cook place three plates on the counter for collection. No sign of Marcus yet. A red-haired woman emerged through the doors of the kitchen backward and swung around, carrying four plates filled with food. She whistled and called out, "Dinner's served."

A nearby table cheered. The atmosphere was addictive and so cheerful. I was fascinated by it. I'd never been to a restaurant or diner where despite how busy they were, everyone seemed to be enjoying themselves.

A sudden explosion of breaking plates shattered through the voices, and I twisted around to the sound. A waitress, slim with short blonde hair and her face covered in freckles, was frantically crouched low, trying to pick up all the broken plate pieces from the floor. A few people watched her, but no one got up to help her.

I didn't think, and the next thing I knew, I was next to her, picking up the mess.

"Oh my god, thank you so much," she whispered nervously, her cheeks stained red from embarrassment.

"It happens," I explained, stacking broken and chipped wedges of ceramic into one hand. I was all too familiar with the fear of breaking things. Alistair made sure to punish me thoroughly if I dropped anything. The punishment tended to come in the form of him using his belt. My skin shivered at the memory, and I hastily picked up more of the mess.

Quickly, I followed the waitress into the kitchen and dumped everything into a trash can in the corner. The setup was simple in the room—a grill against the back wall, with frying baskets off to the side, a chopping counter on this end along with the sink, and metal shelving with bowls and plates filling every other space against the wall. Steaks sizzled on the grill, and it smelled heavenly. The cook stood with his back to us as he seasoned the meat. He wore a bright red bandana over his hair, black jeans, and a bright yellow tank top under a black apron. The man was tall, toned, and moving at a million miles an hour, plating up dishes, his bare arms glistening from the heat.

"You're a blessing," the blonde said and offered me a dish towel to wipe my hands.

I glanced down at her name badge as I cleaned myself off. "It's my job, Eve," I said, trying to joke, which had her looking at me quizzically. "I'm the new waitress Marcus hired, Rune."

Her eyes widened, as did her smile in an excited surprise. "Sweet Jesus, thank you." She threw her arms around me, her hug like iron shackles for someone thinner than me and standing only five foot three. Her reaction took me off guard at first, mostly because I wasn't used to such open affection...and I wasn't a fan of being touched.

"It's been this busy every night for forever, and my feet

are about to drop off. So let's get you out there before we have a mutiny." She giggled, and the sound was adorable, her nose wrinkling slightly in her beaming expression. I hadn't even started work yet, and I was already beginning to get my hopes up about this place... Maybe I'd even make some friends.

I was getting ahead of myself, and it didn't matter since I was leaving anyway, but it would be nice to have some friendly faces around.

She turned and looked around. "Rae, where do you keep the spare aprons?"

The cook turned and came toward us, offering me his hand. "Hey, I'm Rae." His voice was deep and raspy.

When he smiled, all his teeth showed. He had that guy next door kind of look with a soft smile and a relaxed feel about him...but there was something odd about his eyes. A yellow rim surrounded his irises like nothing I'd ever seen before. His nostrils flared as I got closer to him to shake his hand. Strange.

"Welcome to the team, and just remember, forks are the restaurant's version of socks." He broke into a laugh, and I couldn't help but chuckle at his very bad joke.

"You're so lame, Rae. Are you still telling that joke?" Eve rolled her eyes.

"She's new, and that means she hasn't heard any of them." He reached into a nearby shelf and came back with a black apron that he pushed into my hands. "Here you go, and good luck."

"Thank you."

He returned to the grill.

All strapped up, I glanced up just as the red-haired woman from earlier burst into the room. My gaze went straight to her name badge on her black shirt. Licia. She had wild red hair with curls that refused to be tamed and the deepest green eyes. She was maybe in her mid to late twenties and had the most beautiful complexion of clear, milky-white skin, a contrast to her ruby lips.

"Why isn't anyone out there?" Her eyes landed on me. "I assume you're the new girl?"

"Yes, I'm Rune. I'm ready to get started."

"Good. I like your eagerness, and you'll need it. For tonight, Eve will take all orders, and you just focus on delivering meals to tables and collecting dirty plates. You think you can handle that? We're short on staff in the bar in the back, so you'll need to pop in there and deliver drinks as well."

"Absolutely." How hard could it be? I was a servant at home, bringing Alistair and his friends meals and drinks all the time, collecting after them, as quickly and quietly as possible. I was well versed in the act of waitressing already. Hopefully.

"Well the food isn't going to serve itself," she called out loudly, clapping her hands, even though she was standing barely a foot away from us.

Eve pushed past me, and I joined her in the main room of the diner, where the voices and music seemed explosive. "Thanks for helping earlier," she whispered. I nodded, already liking her. Especially since she hadn't asked me anything about myself yet. Hopefully, she would keep that up.

"No problem. So, is Licia the owner?"

"She's a co-owner of Moonstruck with her partner, Marcus. Then there's also Wilder. He's the big boss in charge of this place and most of the town. You have to watch out for him. Licia's nice, but she does have a temper on her."

"Good to know. Guess what they say about redheads must be true," I joked.

"Did you know, ancient Greeks believed that redheads turned into vampires when they died?"

Her comment surprised me, and I looked at her. "Where did that come from?"

She smiled shyly. "I'm studying history at an online college, and it's incredible what the ancient Greeks believed." She shrugged nervously. "Everyone tells me I say the strangest things, so just ignore me."

"I wouldn't do that. I like learning new things too."

She smirked, a light blush to her cheeks, and her eyes lit up. Someone yelled out from a nearby table, and she hurried over to see what they wanted. I turned and saw a stack of dirty plates on a nearby booth and got to work.

The evening was passing smoothly. I'd eventually made my way into the back bar section where drinks had collected on the counter to be delivered to the tables. I started reading the orders to work out who got what drink.

"What the hell?" a deep commanding voice came from behind me, so sudden and unexpected that I flinched around, my heart pounding loudly in my ears.

Emerald green eyes stared back at me, fury burning in their depths.

That was what I saw first.

Him staring right into my soul.

Green eyes that belonged to the face of a veritable god... who also happened to be an asshole.

It was the man who'd growled at me in the street and then forced me off the sidewalk for him and his girlfriend to walk past. He was standing there underneath the arched entrance to the bar area. He was intimidatingly large and scowling at me, shadows shifting across his face. Just like when I saw him last, he had his dark hair pushed back, a few strands escaping and falling over one eye, stubble coating his sharp jaw. Dark, heavy eyebrows pulled together as he stared at me with piercing eyes. He wore a navy long-sleeved tee with a V-neck, strong muscles pulling the fabric across his chest, and deep-blue jeans that hugged clearly powerful legs.

How in the world was the asshole still so gorgeous, even as he looked ready to tear me apart with his bare hands?

My heart beat furiously. Suddenly, I forgot everything and even whose drinks I was holding. I reined in my thoughts quickly, everything in me on high alert.

"E-excuse me?"

"You're fired," he stated abruptly, silencing those around us. "We don't need help."

My mouth completely dried up, and I stood shell-shocked at his words. I had no idea who this guy was. Was this some kind of joke to play on the new girl? Eve's words about who the bosses at Moonstruck Diner were hit me then, and like a tsunami, recognition crashed into me.

"Y-you're Wilder?"

"Oh, good, you do have a brain. Now get your things and leave," he snarled. His body was rigid...furious. I wanted to scream.

This had to be a joke. It was complete bullshit in fact. I quickly returned the glasses of drinks in my hands to the bar before I did something stupid like toss them in his face. I swallowed the tangled mess of emotions burning me up from the inside out and blinked away the frustrated tears threatening to fall from my eyes.

Humiliation painted my cheeks as I felt the gaze of everyone in the bar on me, listening to our drama unfold. I'd been pushed around my whole life, so my first instinct was to want to back down and run away. But the day I escaped, I made myself a promise. I would never let anyone shove me around ever again.

"Are you hard of hearing, sweetheart?" he sneered.

I shivered and pushed against my instinct, lifting my chin and looking him in the eyes. Every nerve in my body snapped. "Marcus hired me—"

"I don't give a fuck. I get final say, and you're out," he said stiffly, turning around and grabbing a glass like he was done with the conversation.

Great, now some of the people in the diner were listening too, turning their heads to watch the commotion as they peered through the doorway that separated the diner from the bar.

I cringed, wanting the floor to crack open and swallow me, but I'd also been in far more humiliating situations. There was almost nothing I could go through that would compete with Alistair's actions.

"Will you listen to me?" I started to say desperately, just as Licia stormed into the bar area, brushing right past Wilder to join us.

"Seriously, Wilder? What the hell? Have you seen how busy we are tonight?" she reprimanded sharply, standing toe to toe with him, her red hair seeming to stand on end in her indignation.

"She's not working here, end of story." Wilder's jawline clenched. I couldn't believe his hatred for a complete stranger...for me. He couldn't even bring himself to look at me as he spoke. This was ridiculous.

"I know I'm new to town..." I began. "But I'm a hard worker, I give you my word." I cringed at how frantic I sounded, but when you were scraping the bottom, you weren't above groveling when you had nothing left to lose.

"Wilder, you've seen how busy we are, and between Eve and I, we're not coping on the floor. Rune is good, and she's fast...at least from what I've seen so far. It's what we've been asking for, and you know the last three people *you* hired couldn't keep up with the fast pace."

I swallowed hard and watched the pair, almost feeling their energy buzz down my arms. He stood quite a bit taller than Licia, which was intimidating as fuck, but she somehow was holding her ground.

"Marcus had no right—" Wilder began, but Licia cut him off.

"He was worried we'd lose Eve if we didn't get someone else in here to help. We need her."

Wilder sighed, and in all honesty, if I wasn't so desperate, I would have loved to toss the damn job into his perfect face and tell him to fuck off. Instead, I stood there, waiting, feeling everyone's eyes on us...on me.

If everyone didn't know I was an outsider, I sure as well had a target on my forehead now.

With another heavy sigh like he was being asked to let a murderer work for him, Wilder glanced at me, his lips curled. "I'll give you one shot, only because Licia believes in you, but one screw up, just one, and you're done. Understand?" He swung to Licia. "You handle her."

He turned abruptly and vanished into the diner.

The earlier strength I'd been using to stand tall crashed through me, and I stumbled back into a stool by the bar. "What was that all about?"

He was scary as shit, and Eve's earlier warning about him didn't come close to the truth. I needed a bottle of tequila after that.

"Are you okay?" Licia asked, not answering my question.

"Yes. I just didn't expect him to be like...like that."

She half laughed like this was an everyday occurrence. "You get used to Wilder after a while. He definitely barks and bites, but he isn't an unreasonable man."

I disagreed with that assessment, but I just said, "Thank you."

"Of course. Now back to work and don't let me down." She marched into the diner, where the sudden rise of voices returned too loud. As much as I burned with humiliation and sweat now dripped down my back, I refused to prove him right.

I turned and got to work. If anything, I would show him how amazing I was that he'd beg me to stay. Then I could stick it in his face when I left.

My cheeks still burned from embarrassment as I went over what had just happened.

It couldn't be that I was just from out of town, right? Or was this one of *those* towns where they didn't tolerate outsiders because the locals harbored a horrible secret like worshipping Satan on every new moon or something crazy. I laughed inwardly at the thought, sometimes my imagination was ridiculous.

This would be okay, I reassured myself. My boss was terrible. But I could do this. This was a temporary situation.

For the next three hours, I worked straight, clearing every table, delivering meals so fast that I found myself waiting on Rae to plate up the dishes. As I stood behind the bar near the kitchen window, I took a sip from my bottled water, noticing Wilder watching me from across the table. He stood near the entrance as a small group of customers left the diner.

The hairs on my neck shifted with the way he stared at me. Shadows gathered under his eyes like it infuriated him just seeing me exist.

"Order's up," Rae called from the kitchen, and I turned as he slid two plates loaded down with steak and roasted vegetables.

What amazed me was that nearly every order tonight consisted of various cuts of meat with a side dish. Either there was a special on tonight on the steak dishes, or this town loved their meat.

I quickly delivered the meals and collected the empty glasses from the next table. Taking a moment, I slipped back into the bar and picked up three drinks on a tray for delivery. I delivered them to a booth where three guys maybe in their late twenties sat. They all greeted me with smiles.

That was a change.

Their faces looked familiar. Oh, they were at the bar last night I realized. I remembered them laughing at my comment about all the wolf decorations.

"Wilder didn't tell us he had a new girl on board," the dark-haired man said, while the other two stared at me with newfound interest, like they were seeing me for the first time. Leering was a better word for it actually. It made me uncomfortable, so I just smiled in response and walked away. As I left, one of them called out after me, "Fine ass. Why don't you bend over for us?" All three of them howled with laughter.

I pretended I didn't hear them, but dark memories sprung up in my head. Of Alistair's pack members mocking me, harassing me, saying vulgar things.

I sunk into the shadows near the kitchen as the visions assaulted me. I tried to catch my breath...to stop my racing pulse as a panic attack threatened. I tried to remind myself I'd escaped.

Keep it together. Just keep it together.

When I glanced up, I caught Wilder's eyes on me, his

presence like a blanket, suffocating me, something unreadable in his gaze.

He started coming this way, and my stomach twisted on itself. Loud footfalls hit the wooden floorboards like thunder. He moved with sureness, with the gracefulness of a predator.

My breath rushed past my lips.

The kitchen bell rang like a salvation call, and it ripped me out of my frozen state. Not waiting for Wilder to reach me, I practically ran to the window and collected the next deliveries, shaking myself out of the dark moment.

Wilder shoved his way down a corridor adjacent to the kitchen door, where I assumed his office was, and I breathed easy. For the rest of the night, I worked my ass off, while steering clear of the leering men. I kept glancing up toward the corridor for any sign of Wilder, but he never made a show for the rest of my shift.

Eve kept to herself, doing her job, chatting and laughing with customers...even the three men at the booth.

I couldn't help but feel like they all knew something I didn't, like they weren't exactly acting like themselves around me.

I wanted to believe it was all in my imagination.

But my gut instinct rarely steered me wrong.

*T*he next morning, when I hit the dirt path, I pushed into a jog. I had to run. It didn't feel like a choice ever since arriving here. It was like there was something inside of me calling to me...forcing me to. It intensified every day to the point of madness, compelling me to go, even with the wolf problem this town seemed to have. I couldn't explain it, but my skin seemed to itch insanely with the compulsion to run.

I put it down to anxiety.

Sitting still gave me time to ponder over everything I'd been through, while running distracted me as I had to focus on breathing and not tripping. That had to be it.

Running also offered me the chance to explore the town on the sly. Something still felt off in Amarok, something I couldn't put my finger on.

There was the way people stared at me, the way they were either rude and dismissive, or so obviously fake that it made my skin feel slimy.

What were they so cautious about? With my past...I was the least dangerous person in the world. Not that they would know that. But nothing about me exactly screamed threat.

I shook my head, wondering why I even cared about Amarok's secrets. I'd be out of here soon enough.

I smiled then, thinking about the fact that I'd made one hundred dollars in tips last night at the diner, even after splitting my money with Eve. I'd almost cried when she handed me my share of the tips. It meant I could buy a little food, put some away to pay for my room at the inn, and then put the rest into my savings to pay off my car.

My footsteps pounded into the ground as I pushed myself, enjoying the wind in my hair, feeling better than I had in too long. It didn't seem possible, but running already felt easier, like there was something in the air here that just invigorated my body.

Sunlight tinted the sky in numerous shades of blues and oranges and violets while the long grasses swayed. The whole location was beautiful.

I crossed the large wooden bridge, inhaling the crisp air, wishing once again that I hadn't wasted so much of my life, that I would have left Alistair long ago.

I wished those things even as I still missed him.

I glanced over to the row of small homes alongside the bank on this side of the river. Two locals stood in their yard talking, their eyes on me. That was the other thing. Everyone here was such a gossip. It was like I was in middle school again. They all whispered about me...stared at me.

That kind of behavior definitely made a girl paranoid.

I could handle that though. I just kept reminding myself *this* was heaven compared to where I'd come from.

I ran at a leisurely pace on the track alongside the road. The sun beat on my shoulders, and birds chirped in the trees. Perfection. I made a conscious effort to keep my eyes out, considering the wolf I'd crossed paths with. I wasn't going to go into the woods today but remain close to town, following the curve of the road along the wood's edge.

A sudden and repetitive engine groan grew louder, and I edged farther off the road, twisting around to see who was driving this way.

A black Jeep cruised forward and seemed to slow upon approaching me.

I squinted to get a view of who was driving, but the dark windows and low afternoon sun made that close to impossible.

My initial instinct was to back away quickly from whoever approached me, but that made me look super paranoid, right?

I paused my run, my breath speeding up as the vehicle stopped on the road alongside me. The window slid down, and the first thing I saw were those green eyes that had haunted my dreams since I first saw them. Of course those eyes came with the usual twisted snarl on his lips.

Wilder.

Fuck. What now? After his behavior at the diner yesterday, I vowed to keep as much distance between us as possible...ignoring the fact that certain parts of my body felt differently about his anger than the rest of me did.

I shouldn't feel this blend of foreboding and arousal when we crossed paths, but he managed to bring them out in me. I added that to the mental list I was keeping of all the reasons I hated myself.

Pushing some hair out of my face, I nervously smiled and glanced around, taking note no one else was around.

"Is something wrong?" I asked, my heart pounding against my chest.

With one hand gripping the steering wheel, his knuckles

white from how hard he held it, he studied me. I ignored the voice in my head that told me to bolt out of there. If I intended to stay in town and work at his diner, then I had to find a way to find peace between us...and I really needed to stop cowering in fear every time he was around.

The way he looked at me right now though...with dark heat behind his gaze...it did something to me. His gaze slowly perused my form, going from my tight leggings up to my tank top until it felt like he'd caressed every inch of my body. Butterflies burst inside my stomach, beating their wings, and my gaze kept brushing over his strong forearm from where he had his sleeve rolled up to his elbow. I shouldn't let my mind wander there, but his muscles flexed as I stared transfixed, and all of a sudden, I foolishly was imagining myself in his arms. My breath heightened as I pictured him over me, under me...in me.

Just as quickly as the thoughts came, I shook them away because seriously...what the fuck was wrong with me? Of all people, I shouldn't be picturing anything with Wilder and I. Something must be seriously broken inside me that I had a fascination with assholes.

"You're out here alone," he barked, stating the obvious.

My hackles rose at his tone, the lust I'd felt rapidly dissipating. My response slipped past my lips. "Exactly, I'm out here alone, not in the woods. Is there a problem?"

"I would have thought Jim or Carrie, or even Licia would have warned you about being alone so close to the woods." He didn't look happy in the slightest, and for the life of me, I couldn't work him out. One minute, he wanted to fire me, the next, he sounded like he might care about something happening to me. That couldn't be right.

"You need to trust me on this," he continued, one of his thick eyebrows arching.

Trust? I hated that word. I'd learned early on that when people used it, it meant you should run, as quickly and as far away from them as you could. Just hearing the word made my pulse race with frustration and suspicion.

Wilder was adept at twisting my insides. He seemed to enjoy hanging me out to dry seemingly without a care in the world. In fact, I got the feeling he enjoyed making me suffer.

"It almost sounds like you care," I answered, sarcastically. "But I'm not afraid of wild animals, at least not during the day. Is there something else I should be worried about?"

He hadn't stopped staring at me, hell, I wasn't even sure that he'd blinked since pulling up. A flare of worry wormed through my gut that I'd chewed off more than I could handle. I got the impression Wilder was so much more than he appeared. There was an air of danger choking the air around him that had all my senses on high alert.

What if he fired me again for talking back to him just now? I mean, that was stupid, but I wouldn't put it past him.

"If this is your attempt to scare me out of town, you should know, monsters and urban legends don't scare me," I murmured when he didn't respond. It was true, I knew that the monsters you should be scared of weren't the ones that your mother told you about at night. The ones you needed to be scared of were the ones your mother willingly pushed you towards, the ones hiding in plain sight.

I let my gaze slide over to his broad chest. My gaze seemed to make his breaths speed up. I stiffened, suddenly imagining him getting out of the car and forcing me to get in with him to take me back into town. That would be something he'd do.

"There are far worse things than monsters out here. You should be careful when you stumble into someone else's backyard, Rune."

With those foreboding words, he hit a button on his door, and the window slid back up, stealing him from my sight. Not a second passed, and he drove down the road, disappearing around the bend of the road that took him into the actual woods.

I fought the anger he awoke in me. "Who the hell do you think you are?" I called out to no one except the woods surrounding me. It suddenly felt like a million eyes were watching me, and I shivered standing there, hating that he'd shattered the little bit of peace I'd managed to grab for myself this afternoon.

Fuck him.

I kept staring in the direction he drove, as if daring him to turn around so I could actually tell him everything I thought about him. Sighing at my stupidity, I shook my head and started running again. No matter what he threw at me, I was better off in this town. I'd adapt and ignore him.

I swung around and started running back closer to town and away from wherever he'd been heading. I made my way quickly...well, as much as my lungs would allow, when the crunch of twigs echoed from the woods behind me as if the universe had decided to prove Wilder right about being out here alone.

I peered over my shoulder, but there was no one there, just the sunlight pouring through the canopy of trees. A strange silence fell over the landscape though. No birds. No wind.

Just me and my breath quickening. I dug my hand into my pocket and pulled out the small mace I'd had in there. I'd purchased it in town right before my run...just in case of those wild animals I claimed not to be afraid of.

I gripped it, my hand shaking.

"Please don't let Wilder be right," I whispered.

I leapt back into a run and made my way closer to town, well aware that running wasn't a good thing when it came to predators. But I wasn't about to lay down and pretend to be dead either.

The crunch came again, closer that time, and I twisted my head in the direction of the woods farther across the road, swearing I'd just seen a shadow flitter amid the trees.

No, I must have imagined it.

My heart raced, and the hairs on my arms lifted. I choked on the trepidation curling inside my chest, but I kept going, pushing one leg in front of the other, refusing to freeze over. I could just picture it now, Wilder coming to the hospital after I was attacked and singing his *I told you* song.

No thank you.

It was probably just a squirrel, or a bunny... Lots of things lived in the forest. It was at times like these that I wished I possessed any of my wolf senses and wolf abilities. Not many things dared to stand up to wolves.

I kept checking over my shoulder as I ran when a snarl rolled from up ahead of me.

I swung my head back to the road, my hand with the mace raised, ready to use. The town lay up ahead, but my attention fell on a figure on the ground at the side of the road.

My heart catapulted right into my throat.

Powdery white and gray fur fluttered in the light breeze on the wolf lying on its side.

The animal half-whimpered, half-snarled, its head lifting as if attempting to pull itself up. Then it collapsed back down. The cries it made broke my heart. I loved all animals, and I couldn't stand by to see any of them harmed, even an apex-predator.

I moved closer with short steps, trying to make enough sound to grab its attention and avoid spooking it further.

Its large head swiveled in my direction once again with haunted looking pale blue eyes that I'd never be able to forget. They were almost human-like, seeming to implore me for help. The animal kept looking into the woods and back at me as if trying to tell me something, but when I scanned the area, I saw nothing.

"What happened to you?" I stepped closer, hugging myself, my muscles tense, ready for me to bolt at a moment's notice should the animal leap to its feet. Except the closer I got, the clearer the issue came to light.

It sported a huge gaping wound across its back leg, blood dripping into the fur and onto the ground. The closer I looked, the worse the injury appeared, and I was certain I could see down to bone.

"Oh, crap. That really looks really bad. What bit you?" I gasped and terror traveled up my spine that something really was roaming these woods. What kind of creature could take a bite like that out of a wolf? Standing about five feet away, I noticed the trail of blood leading right into the woods from where the wolf must have dragged itself out here. Why would a wild animal come to the road?

The wild look in its eyes touched me in a way I never expected, and I knew exactly what I had to do.

"I'll be right back, I promise I won't leave you out here." I felt stupid talking out loud like it could understand me, but it was helping me to stay at least a little bit calm as my mind raced with what to do.

Those big eyes remained on me, and I cringed each time I looked at his back leg and how badly it had been mangled. It was terrifying to think about what could have done that. Another wolf maybe?

Wilder's words swirled in my mind.

I took one last look at the poor wolf, then back into the woods. If something really was watching us, would the wolf even be here by the time I returned with help?

I turned and ran faster than I thought possible, my skin crawling, never once looking back.

I darted over the bridge and pushed myself up toward the main road flanked by stores. I remember spotting a doctor's office a few days ago. I somehow doubted a town this small would have a veterinary, so a normal doc would have to do.

The blinds on the doctor's office window were shut, but I tried the door anyway, breathing a sigh of relief when it opened. I hurried inside as I tucked my mace back into my pocket. I was breathing so heavily, I drew everyone's attention. For all they knew, I might have come in here suffering from a heart attack with how much I was huffing and puffing.

White. That was all I saw at first. White walls, reception counter, chairs, and even the television playing on mute was white.

"Are you all right?" the receptionist asked, wide eyed as if I'd startled her. She struggled up from her seat, and I had the random thought that her white scrubs probably weren't smart in a doctor's office.

An older woman sitting on the row of chairs against the window stared at me with disdain. I did a double take to ensure I was seeing right. Under her gaze, I felt like a bug under a microscope. She held onto a wide-brimmed yellow hat and was crushing the brim like she was anxious.

I drew in rushed breaths, trying to calm them as I stumbled toward the counter. "I-I'm f-fine." Gasping for air, I kept going. "I think I just ran a mile in five minutes."

Laughter came from the woman in the waiting chair. "Oh dear, you are very out of shape if you're barely catching your breath from just one mile."

I stiffened, but couldn't argue with her. *I was out of shape, but a five-minute mile would be hard for anyone, lady*, I thought indignantly. She wore a floral dress past her knees and had to be in her late fifties with her short, wavy hairstyle. I bet she couldn't make that run in five minutes. Even if she was on the thinner side. She watched me with a scowl, and I put it down to her being in the *hating the newcomer* camp.

I didn't waste my breath on her and returned my attention to the receptionist. She had blonde hair pulled off her face and in a ponytail...and she wasn't glaring at me. So that was a plus. She sat back in her chair behind the counter, seeing that I wasn't about to die.

"Did you want to make an appointment?" she asked.

"No. There's a wolf near the woods, and it's injured. Something attacked it, and the poor thing is bleeding very badly. Could the doctor maybe—"

"Where?" the busy-body woman asked, placing her hat on the chair next to her and getting to her feet. "What sort of wolf?" She stepped closer, practically standing in my face.

I backed up. "It was a wolf, a gray one."

"Greta," the receptionist warned.

The older woman's nostrils flared with her exasperated exhale to keep quiet. Was this woman some kind of animal lover? She seemed very invested.

"I'm sorry but we're not an animal hospital," the receptionist answered.

I turned to her. "Is there a vet in town?" I quipped.

She shook her head, and I wanted to laugh out loud. "Surely, the doctor can help out the poor animal then? It's bleeding on the side of the road after pulling itself from in the woods for help."

"You were in the woods alone?" she asked, and I sighed. What was wrong with everyone in this town?

"What sort of bite?" Greta asked.

These were not the normal kind of questions people asked in such a situation.

The door alongside the reception counter suddenly opened, and a young man stepped out wearing a hoodie, his gaze low, shoulders curled forward as if he'd just received the worst news in the world.

When he looked up, I stiffened.

Daniel. I remembered him from when he rushed into the inn all panicked and talking about blood.

Greta abruptly scoffed and glared at Daniel like she might pierce him alive with her stare.

"What now?" he asked, giving her an exasperated scowl like he might break into an argument.

She was fuming, tucking her handbag under her arm as she grabbed her hat. "What did you do now?" She swiftly marched right out the door, with Daniel right on her heels, saying, "What are you talking about?"

"That was strange," I whispered under my breath.

"Oh, don't pay Greta any attention. She's always in everyone's business but she means well. Did you know she took Daniel into her home when he lost his parents years ago?"

Part of me felt a hint of sympathy for Daniel, when I caught the doctor emerging from his office. He was a super old man, sun spots on his skin, thinning white hair, and walking rather quickly for someone who looked like they neared a hundred years old.

"Excuse me," I asked with a soft voice. "I found an

injured wolf just in the woods. Would you be able to help him or know who could help?"

The man's head lifted, his gaze meeting mine, swimming with something so sympathetic and caring in his expression, I automatically liked him.

He exchanged looks with the receptionist who said, "You have an appointment in ten minutes."

He clapped his hands. "Then that's plenty of time."

Despite her heavy sigh, the doctor turned my way. "Let me know exactly where you found him, and I'll take it from here."

"Are you sure we should be doing this?" the reception asked, interrupting us.

"Just grab my bag and car keys." Then he looked back at me, waiting for my response.

In one breath, I told him everything about the injured wolf, and then in a flash, they were on their way, locking the door behind us as we all left.

"Now that was super strange," I mumbled to myself as they both hopped into a car and sped off in the direction I'd just come from without another word. I made a note to swing past the office tomorrow and check on the wolf's status.

I turned and made my way up the main road, deciding that something odd was definitely happening in this town... something everyone was privy too except me. And it had everything to do with the surrounding woods and the wolves. I felt it in my bones.

*T*he floorboards thumped beneath my feet from the music downstairs in the inn. I combed my wet hair off my face, having every intention of heading downstairs. The diner had burst with customers earlier today, and I'd been run off my feet, so exhausted, I could barely stand. But instead of crashing into bed after my shift, I wanted a drink to wind down. Plus, the sound of the commotion downstairs had me curious to find out what was going on.

I'd seen too many strange things in my short time in town to put it down to some pure coincidence. Thinking through things today, I'd decided it made sense that with very little tourists in town, this place had become isolated. It was why they were protected from outsiders. If they'd been alone this long, anyone might come across as a threat to their simple way of life. I just had to show them I wasn't a threat.

I'd bought a pair of black heels for the job interviews I'd hoped for when I was fleeing Alistair's pack. I stepped into them now, gazing at myself critically in the mirror one last time. The A-line dress with spaghetti straps fell mid-thigh, cinched in at my waist and laced up across my chest. What I loved about this dress when I bought it had been the color. A faded, summery yellow that reminded me of the outdoors. I'd seen it at the same store as where I'd bought the shoes, and I just had to have it. Alistair never would have allowed me to wear something so bright...and revealing. It represented hope when I saw it hanging there. I kind of couldn't believe I was actually getting to wear it.

I reached for the necklace my mother had given me, the only gift I had left from her. I hadn't been able to convince myself to throw it away, even after all these years. A sterling silver chain with a luna pendant. The sickle of the moon more specifically, a symbolism of life and death, my mother had told me. Something to empower me, she'd said at the time. I laughed at the thought. I was only wearing it now because the dress needed something to fill the open space over my chest.

I obviously was well versed in lying to myself.

"You can do this," I whispered as I put the necklace on, then headed downstairs, preparing myself for all the stares. But this was all part of my plan, the more people saw me, the more they would get used to me and stop making me feel like a freak all the time. This would help them too, because they really needed to learn staring was rude.

But once I reached the base of the stairs, I froze on the bottom step because I wasn't expecting this.

The place was packed. People on every chair, others standing by the wall, chatting, and some near the eating section that had been cleared and now sported a pool table. How in the world did Jim and Carrie bring that thing in there?

And where were all of these people the night I arrived?

A rock song played in the background to all the voices, and I licked my dry lips, forcing myself to not head back upstairs from how out of place I felt. The strong smell of aftershave and perspiration made for an interesting smell that almost overpowered my senses. Almost...

It was mostly guys, but the few females who mingled with them wore simple jeans, low-cut tops, and I felt extremely overdressed in that moment, sticking out like a sore thumb.

Breathing hard, I started to sense their eyes on me, and slowly, more seemed to notice my presence. I cursed myself internally for wearing a yellow dress. What had I been thinking?

"You look scared." A short, built man with a long beard strolled my way from a table with three others, all staring my way. My heart beat so fast, and I was certain my cheeks burned up. He gave me a sickly-sweet grin.

I retreated up one step, unsure I could do this, reminded too much of the men in Alistair's pack who thought it was okay to hit on me in front of everyone else just to rouse a reaction out of me. To humiliate me, to get Alistair to treat me like garbage for their amusement.

"Back off, Jarrod," Jim said, suddenly appearing from around the corner of the staircase, carrying a tray of beers. He looked my way, offering me a lighthearted smile. "Head to the bar, darlin'. Carrie will get your first drink on the house."

I used that moment to slip away from the bearded man who had his friends heckling him. They looked like they could easily belong in a biker gang. In fact, half the men had that similar look to them. Rugged, tough, and wearing lots of denim. Most of them were hanging around the pool table, and only when the crowd parted, did my eyes land on Daxon.

My breath caught in my throat. He raked his hand through his blond hair, standing across the pool table, watching the game. In his other hand, he held a bottle of beer, dressed in jeans and a grey henley top so tight, his muscles couldn't be missed.

He suddenly burst into a strong, loud laugh that sent a delicious buzz through my body.

A sense of anticipation and excitement flooded me, my nerves sparking at the sound. It made me feel alive. It was nothing I'd ever experienced before, but everything I wished I would have had with Alistair. Instead, my fated mate had done everything he could to kill whatever spark he'd seen in me.

My life had been ugly and violent, and it had been all I knew for too long. I would always bear the scars.

With that thought, I looked away from the golden god and turned to the bar with an empty seat by the counter as if it was cleared just for me. Jumping up onto it, I swiveled toward Carrie, who slid a drink in front of me before I even ordered one.

"The house specialty," she said. "Stinging Breeze. Bitters, bourbon, tonic, and a squeeze of orange juice with a dash of sugar."

"Sounds good." I accepted the drink and took a sniff, the orange coming through strongly, so I took a sip. Sweetness coated my tongue, followed by a hit of fire rushing down my throat. I coughed, close to spurting out what I'd drank.

Carrie laughed. "The more you drink, the less it burns."

I wasn't too sure about that theory, but I said my thanks and spun on the chair to face the room while holding my drink, hating the sensation of having my back unprotected. My attention again swept over to Daxon, holding the cue stick, leaning over the table to take his shot. It was too bad he wasn't facing the other direction, giving me a perfect view of that gorgeous ass. That was the kind of relaxing night I wanted.

"You're so obvious," a female voice purred in my ear.

I snapped around, my drink sloshing over the rim and running down my fingers and onto my thigh.

"Oh, hell." I quickly put the glass on the bar and grabbed a napkin to wipe the mess, then looked up to come face to face with a dark-haired beauty. The same one who'd been with Wilder on the sidewalk days ago. And now she was in my personal space, studying me with an expression I couldn't work out.

"Sorry, what?" I asked.

"Don't worry, every girl in town dreams about claiming that piece of walking sex. And damn, he fucks like a demon, trust me." She winked at me like we were friends, smirking and biting her lip, before glancing over at Daxon. "Oh and here's a tip. Try not to look so desperate when you stare at him. It's really pitiful to watch." Her fake friendliness melted away into a mocking sorrowful expression.

All right...so the girl was a bitch. Good to know.

"I don't know what you're talking about," I replied, refusing to engage with her.

"Listen here, you little piece of shit," she hissed suddenly as she leaned closer, her hand gripping my arm, fingernails digging into flesh.

Fire erupted within me, and I pushed her arm off me, shocked at what was happening. "Excuse me?"

She didn't back away, her angry features warping her beauty and transforming her into an ugly hag.

Her gaze dipped down my body then, and she paused on my chest, physically flinching from me suddenly like I might have leprosy. "You're wasting your time by putting your luck in that," she growled before releasing me.

I blinked at her, utterly confused as I glanced down at my moon necklace and then back up. But she was already sauntering across the room, her hips swaying. Her cut-off denim Daisy Dukes barely covered her ass, and every guy in the place made sure to stare.

Well, okay. I was putting her firmly in the crazy column.

I couldn't escape her words about Daxon though. They kept circling through my mind like vultures.

He fucks like a demon.

Here I thought she was with Wilder, but maybe I'd been mistaken.

I hated her in that moment, more than I did when I'd seen her with Wilder. She walked over to Daxon and draped an arm around his shoulders...like she owned him. A spear of sharp jealousy drove right through my middle, licking and burning at my insides. I took a long drink, wanting to wash away what I was feeling...or at least numb it, but the sweet taste had soured.

The guy on the stool next to me, glanced over. "You could always challenge her for him. We haven't had a good cat fight in here in too long." He leered at me, smiling and revealing one of his missing front teeth.

Eeww.

"I have no idea what you're saying."

He shrugged and went back to nursing his drink.

When I looked back up, the voices seemed to fall silent, only the music filling the void. I glanced around quickly to work out what was happening.

My gaze fell on Wilder, and my stomach tightened. Where did he come from? He stood a few feet away from Daxon dressed in dark pants that encased his powerful legs and a blue button-up shirt that was taut from the way his biceps were flexing as he clenched his fists angrily.

Both him and Daxon were arguing, the anger twisting their expressions. All the while, the dark-haired woman stood between them, a hand on each of their chests, except she didn't look one bit upset. She smiled like she was the happiest person in the world, like she might be getting off on having the guys fight over her. Were they fighting over her? What exactly was going on between those three anyway?

All of a sudden, she ducked, and Wilder threw the first

punch, clipping Daxon just below his left eye, sending him sprawling backward onto the pool table. The viciousness of the attack took me off guard. I exhaled rapidly, feeling my chest curl in on itself.

My heart soared at how quickly this escalated from argument into a fight.

Daxon snapped back up quicker than I'd ever seen anyone move, and he threw himself at Wilder, both of them stumbling until Wilder hit the wall.

Then the room exploded with cheers and hoots, the crowd shoving to get closer to the battle.

My pulse pounded quickly as everything escalated into chaos.

Jim and Carrie were trying to push themselves into the crowd, to clearly break up the fight, while no one else did a thing. Except now I couldn't see a single thing.

Quickly, I rushed over to a nearby chair and climbed on it for a better view over the many heads.

The black-haired woman, who had definitely started this, sat on the pool table cross-legged, clapping and laughing like a mad person. Wilder and Daxon were now on the ground, rolling around. All I could see were flying punches, really making it close to impossible to see who was winning.

These two were all male, all alpha. There was no other way to describe them, and I watched them in a strange amusement. A tingle started deep in my stomach, diving deeper at seeing them battle. I shouldn't feel anything but shock at their behavior, and here I buzzed from a rising desire through me. Geez, was I any better than the crazy chick?

There was something so intoxicating, so alluring, about watching them fight.

The music never stopped, and it almost seemed like they fought to the rhythm. Both were back on their feet, Wilder with a busted lip, Daxon bleeding from the cut under his eye.

Jim jutted between them in a wild attempt that was honestly risking his life, his arms flailing about, but the pair didn't even notice. They just lunged at each other once again, ending up on the pool table.

The dark-haired girl squealed as she rapidly scurried out of their way, which made me laugh quietly to myself.

Punch after punch. These two were extraordinary, taking so many hits but neither falling over. Each of them was muscular, towering over almost everyone in the room. It was obvious they were dangerous as hell. To see them collide like that was like a train wreck where I just couldn't look away. How long could they go on like this, anyway?

The girl who'd instigated this caught my attention from across the room. She was watching me, not the action, and something in her expression changed. It became almost feral like the madness in the air tonight was contagious. A darkness swept over my eyes, sending a shiver down my spine.

In that exact moment, Jim whistled so loud, it drew even Wilder and Daxon's attention to him.

"That's fucking enough," he bellowed. "You want to rip yourselves apart, go outside for it. Take your asses out of here now! Everyone, out."

At first, no one moved, and I had no idea if Jim held such a command over the rowdy crowd. Everyone's eyes were on the two powerhouses in the middle of the bar. Their shirts torn and stained with blood, their strong chests rising and falling rapidly with each breath. They exchanged glares, and it was clear these two held deep hatred for one another.

Daxon turned away first, then Wilder did the same, both going in opposite directions. The masses then dispersed, all coming my way.

Panicked, I rapidly hopped down from the chair I'd been standing on. In seconds, I was engulfed by bodies pushing past, all shoving to get out the door.

Elbows in my side, the huge men barely noticed I stood in their way as they nudged me left and right. Escape seemed impossible when everywhere I turned, more and more bodies made a rush for the exit.

I maneuvered my way past a few people, when the heavy stench of perspiration hit me so hard, it made me faint. The smell was anything but pleasant, and it swallowed me, stirring my panic. An alarm flared through me that I couldn't get away from them, couldn't breathe.

The bearded man emerged from the mass, leering at me, his hand on my neck so fast, I barely had time to react.

Ice filled my veins at the way he looked at me with all the wrong intentions.

But just as quick as he reached for me, he screeched, flinging his arm from me as if he'd touched acid. He ripped my necklace off as he fell. And in that exact moment, his arm appeared clawed, fingers tipped with razor-sharp nails.

I screamed, backing away.

He scrambled off the floor and then pressed himself into the masses, vanishing while the wave of bodies kept me imprisoned.

Fuck, what the hell was that? I couldn't think straight, but I hastily bent over and picked up my torn necklace, barely avoiding getting my hand trampled.

When I stood up, I found myself crammed and squeezed right outside the door with the flock, my heart beating frantically. I finally burst free from their cluster, stumbling to freedom, sucking in fresh air as I pushed the impending panic attack away. Frantically, I scanned the area for the bearded man to see if I was going insane and seeing things now.

No sign of him.

Shit, did I really just see his hand transform into claws?

The group from the pub trampled over the lawn and made their way either over the bridge or toward the homes on this side of the river. Only faint lights from nearby buildings pierced the darkness.

Sweat dripped down my neck from how hot it had become in there, not that it made a huge difference being out here as there was nothing timid about the heat outside either.

I started heading back inside, wanting to reach my room and lock the door. My head remained too blurred to make sense of what exactly I'd seen and if it had been all in my imagination. Before I reached the door, a shadow fell over me, and I tensed that the man had returned.

I twisted around quickly, dread tightening around me.

But it was Wilder who stood in from me. I should have been relieved, but how could I be when he was standing there, bloody from the fight, his face perfectly expressionless? I stumbled back a few steps, remembering the power he carried. I wasn't exactly in the mood for a lesson from him on the dangers of being outside in the dark, since it was kind of his fault I was out here in the first place.

"Did you enjoy the fight?" he growled out. He picked up a lock of my hair, then leaned forward and inhaled deeply.

Nothing about Wilder made sense to me, and I shoved his hand off me. "Sure, I love when grown men act like children," I said with a scoff.

His nose wrinkled, while that spark deep inside me

erupted, tearing me in two directions, the battle between hating and desiring this guy buzzing around inside of me.

When he stepped closer, I backed away several steps, until my heels hit the stone wall of the inn.

I glanced over to the door, only three feet away. "I'll scream if you try anything."

"Go ahead," he prompted, pitching both hands on the wall over my shoulders, caging me in. The breeze smothered me in his scent, a blend of faint cologne, his masculine, woodsy smell, and something almost earthy. Regardless, the way he smelled shouldn't have turned me on or made me imagine what his lips tasted like, but damn, it did.

"You're going to regret coming here." His gaze traced every inch of my face, pausing on my lips, his mouth parting slightly.

My breath caught in my throat while a dangerous look crossed his face. "I—It's not like I had much choice," I murmured back, frozen to the wall.

"You have no idea what you've walked into."

I swallowed hard as he pulled back, and I followed him, desperate suddenly to know what he was talking about.

"What do you mean?" I called after him.

But he only merged into the shadows, completely vanishing from my sight. And then he was gone without a sound.

I was alone.

The hairs on my arms stood on end, and I suddenly didn't feel safe outside.

I turned and ran inside the inn.

*L*ast night had been fucking crazy.

There was no other way to put it. I shook my head, remembering the claw I thought I saw. Maybe this town was making me crazy too.

I'd just gotten out of the shower, and I stood in front of the mirror brushing my hair that fell almost all the way to my ass. As a child, I'd always hated the color. It was such a light shade of blonde that it was almost white. I'd been called "albino" and "freak" more times than I could count growing up. I'd had to ask my mom what albino even meant the first time I'd heard it. Her hair was a rich, russet color, and I'd always wished she'd passed it on to me. Evidently, the father that I'd never met had black hair, so apparently, I was an anomaly. Just another lucky thing about my life.

The comments had faded over time though, and the pendulum had swung the opposite way where my hair gave me too much attention from the male population. There'd even been a time I'd been considered the hot girl at school. I laughed bitterly at the thought.

I was a far cry from that now.

Haunted blue eyes that were too big for my face stared back at me in the mirror. I continued to study myself as I went over last night's events and continued to critique myself. I fingered the edges of my frayed hair, not able to stop myself from comparing my looks to the crazy chick from last night. When was the last time I'd done something like put on makeup or style my hair? When was the last time I'd cared?

There was that hair salon down the street. I could go there. Just for a little trim. And even though I was supposed to be saving every cent, I needed something to make me feel better about myself. I hadn't cared what I looked like for a long time. What was the point when the person you loved the most in the world despised you?

Maybe I would dye it. Start totally fresh. Yes, I would do that.

Excited about the possibilities of shedding the past...at least physically, I hurried and got dressed. After I left the inn, I decided to stop by the doctor's office on the way to the salon to check on the wolf from yesterday. Hopefully, they'd actually gone to help it.

On the sidewalk, I almost ran into a man who was walking with his head down. I stuttered to a halt when he clipped my shoulder and lifted his head to look at me. Pale blue eyes stared into mine. He quickly looked away and hurried past.

But those eyes stayed with me.

They looked just like the injured wolf's eyes from yesterday. I was seeing things because I was subconsciously worried about how he was doing, I told myself.

But I was beginning to suspect that I wasn't crazy.

I busted into the doctor's office similar to yesterday, and once again, scared the receptionist. She held her chest and took a deep breath, laughing nervously when she saw who it was.

"You're a ferocious little thing, aren't you," she commented before giving me a practiced smile. "How can I help you today?"

I shifted awkwardly in place. "I was just wondering how the wolf from yesterday was doing."

Her smile fell for a second before she quickly replaced it. "It's fine. Already released back into the wild. The bite wasn't bad at all, nothing to be concerned with."

I gaped at her, unsure if I was hearing her right. I knew what I'd seen. And it hadn't been "nothing to be concerned with."

"Anything else I can help you with?" she asked politely, obviously wanting me to leave.

I shook my head and mumbled a goodbye as I left the office very confused. That weird feeling in my gut was back. I walked to the salon, lost in my head.

Shaking the tingles I was feeling off, I looked through the glass door of the salon and saw the redhead that I'd seen before working on an older woman with silver streaked blonde hair. A little bell on the door announced my entrance as I opened the door and walked in. The redhead's eyes lit up when she saw me. "Oh Lordy, you're here. I was fixing to come hunt you down if I didn't see you in the next week. I've been dying to work on your hair since the first moment I saw you," she all but squealed. She was holding a spray bottle in her hand she'd been spraying on her client's hair, and in her exuberance, she sprayed water all over the woman's face.

"Whoops!" she hollered as she grabbed a tissue from the work station in front of her and dabbed the water off. Her client rolled her eyes but didn't seem surprised at the accident.

I couldn't help but grin, a move that was surprisingly becoming easier and easier after a few days of doing it. The wolf slipped out of my mind.

"You settle yourself down right there while I finish Gloria up, and then we'll get to work. I'll be done in a jiffy, ya hear?" she ordered.

I meekly nodded and then sat down on one of the comfy padded chairs that were set up against the wall. While the two women chatted back and forth, I looked around the place. It was definitely catered towards women. Muted pinks, silvers, and blacks were all over the place, creating a sleek modern feel that was a bit out of place in this town with all of its quaint architecture. There were three stations set up, pink chairs in front of Hollywood style mirrors with the big bulbs. And black frames were set up on some of the walls, featuring old black and white movie posters.

I loved it.

I was so lost in my observations, I didn't notice that she was finished until she snapped her fingers in front of me as she passed by to check out her customer.

"Go ahead and get yourself settled in that chair. We'll get to work in just a minute."

"Okay," I said softly, feeling shy in the face of her exuberance as I switched chairs.

She checked the woman out and then grabbed a broom and started sweeping up the hair lying on the black tiled floor. "I like the black aesthetic, but it certainly shows everything," she complained as she finished up.

I nodded like I knew anything about aesthetic or design in general. She gave me a grin, showcasing two front teeth that had a slight gap in between them, giving her an extra dose of charm. Her hair was big and curly, fitting the Southern twang she had going, and she had freckles lightly peppering the bridge of her nose.

She held out a hand in front of me, and I shook it awkwardly. "Miyu," she commented.

"What?" I asked, confused.

"Miyu, that's my name," she said with another wide grin. "It's weird, I know."

"I like it," I told her. "It's unique."

"Unique," she repeated, appearing to savor the word on her tongue. "I'm going to start using that."

"Most people think my name's going to be Darla or Dolly, something fitting these large hooters of mine," she explained as she put a silver cape around my neck, gesturing to her chest, which was indeed larger than the average woman's. "I wish I could say my mother was drunk on moonshine when she came up with it, but apparently, the name came from my older brother, who was one at the time, mind you. My mother swears on her life that he pointed at her stomach and said 'Miyu.' He was of course babbling because he was a baby, but you could never convince her otherwise."

I giggled as I envisioned the scene in my head. "Didn't your dad have anything to say about it?"

"My father was a smart man. When you're married to a woman like my mother, you learn to give in to her craziness. Happy wife, happy life as they say."

I snorted at the phrase. I'd heard it. I'd just never seen it in action. "My name's Rune," I told her.

"Ah," she said. "So you know all about 'unique' names then."

"I'm an expert," I replied, and she let out a horse like snort.

"All right, so what are you thinking today?" she asked as she dragged her bright pink painted fingernails through my hair.

"I was thinking dark, like a dark brown or something," I blurted out, still set on a major change.

"Nope and nope," she commented as she pushed me up and began to lead me towards the sinks which were set up on one of the walls.

"What?" I asked, sure I hadn't heard her right.

"Girl, this hair was given to you by the gods. No way am I touching it with any color. We are going to give you a nice cut though. You kind of look like one of those polygamist chicks. No offense," she added as an afterthought as she began to wash my hair.

A loud laugh erupted out of me, and I quickly covered my mouth, shocked at the sound. When was the last time I'd laughed like that, so hard that it had reached into my stomach?

"Do you tell all your clients what to do?" I asked after I'd stopped laughing.

"No, but I tell my friends what to do all the time. And I think that's what we're going to be."

I'd gone from laughing to trying to hold in a sob at the sweet statement. Talk about whiplash.

"I'd like that," I said quietly.

She hummed, pretending to ignore the emotion in my voice as she washed my hair. My eyes slipped close as she massaged my scalp, and a little humming sound came out of my mouth which she thankfully ignored.

It was over too soon, and then she led me back to the chair with a large towel wrapped around my head.

"Stunning," she murmured as she began to comb out my hair. "So, where are you visiting us from?"

I tensed at the question. "Chicago," I finally said, figuring there was no harm in telling her.

She froze for a second, her eyes flashing strangely as I watched her in the mirror. It was only a moment's pause, and then she continued on as if nothing was wrong.

"This is probably a bit different for you then," she finally said as she picked up her scissors and started to get to work. I watched with butterflies as pieces of my hair fell to the ground.

"Very," I agreed, wishing I could say just how much it differed.

I told her about the tree incident and the animal that had passed in front of my car. "Do you have a pack nearby?" I asked her. "I hear them every night."

She smiled as if I'd said something funny, and that strange feeling started in my chest again. "There are actually two packs here," she informed me. "I'm sure you've been warned not to be out at night alone."

"I have," I told her, a little shocked and scared at her words.

"Is everyone all right with having that many wolves around?"

This time she outright laughed, and I knew she was party to some kind of joke at my expense right now.

This town was weird.

"I'm pretty sure they're okay with it," she finally answered. "Has everyone been okay to you? There are lots of strong personalities here."

"It's been a mixed bag," I muttered, biting my lip just thinking about Wilder...and Daxon. I blurted out the whole story with Wilder, and by the end, she was laughing so hard that she could barely stand.

"Be careful with those," I told her wide-eyed as her scissors barely missed stabbing my head in her exuberance.

She straightened up and wiped a tear from her eye. "That's Wilder, all right. He's an asshole, but he has good intentions. He owns half of this town, and he rarely steers us wrong."

I mulled over that. I'd known he owned the diner...but half the town?

"I met a man named Daxon as well. He and Wilder don't seem to get along."

She pursed her lips like she'd tasted something sour. "Those two have hated each other almost since the moment they sprung from the womb. Arcadia just made it worse."

"Arcadia?" I asked, knowing immediately she was talking about the raven-haired beauty who had it out for me.

"They've both been in love with her for as long as I can remember. She's always been the it girl round here, if you know what I mean."

I nodded before remembering she was trying to cut my hair, and she gave me that small, strange smirk again. Jealousy threaded through my insides thinking of her with them. I felt feverish just thinking about it actually.

"Arcadia loved that attention. I mean, who wouldn't though? Having two men who look like that at your beck and call. She dated both of them on the sly. Told each of them she was giving up her virginity to them. It was a big scandal when Wilder and Daxon found out about each other."

"So they dropped her, right?"

Miyu just shook her head, disgust carved into her features. "Daxon loved her. Wilder too, but Daxon...well, you've met him. He's a sweetheart. Totally fell for her weak ass explanations. Everyone told him to drop that girl. But love makes men fools. Plus, he was getting it on the regular, and I hear Arcadia's an animal in the sack." She snorted to herself, as if she'd said something funny.

The jealousy had become flat-out hate as unbidden thoughts of Arcadia and Daxon wrapped around each other flashed through my mind.

"And Wilder?"

"Hates her guts."

"I saw them just the other day though. And he definitely did not seem like he hated her."

She raised an eyebrow at that news. "Well, that's a new occurrence."

"So are she and Daxon still together?" I asked hesitantly, trying to come across as just curious, but I knew Miyu could see through me all too easily.

Miyu sighed, her shoulders drooping at my question. "Arcadia broke that boy's heart. Rumor is she got pregnant with his baby...and then got rid of it without even telling him about it. Daxon went through a wild streak after that, screwing a bunch of women, but I think he's through that now."

My mouth dropped open in shock, even as an unbidden thought of my own stomach rounded with a tanned hand on top of it struck me.

I was crazy. It was official.

"That's just a rumor though, right?"

"There's always a lot of truth to rumors in this town, Rune. And I have no doubt that rumor's the real deal. Arcadia would never allow herself to be burdened with anything like a child, even if it was Daxon's...or Wilder's."

"Daxon owns the other half of the town, and Arcadia almost made him lose everything. We all hate the bitch, but she continues to prance around like she's the ruler of us all." Miyu's tone dripped with venom every time she mentioned Arcadia's name. "She thinks she still owns them, and maybe she does, but I'd love to see them get away from her." She looked at me meaningfully, raising her eyebrows in a way that I didn't understand.

I frowned, thinking over her story. "Daxon and Wilder seem a little young to own any part of any town. They've got to be what...mid-twenties?"

She snorted again, and there was that small weird smile. "Daxon and Wilder's families both founded this town back in the day. Leadership in this town is sort of passed down the family tree, if ya know what I mean."

A thought hit me then, one that left acid on my tongue. "Have you screwed Daxon?" I blurted out.

Miyu threw back her head like that was the funniest thing she'd ever heard. "I've got a man. And he doesn't share. Not that I do either. I'd cut his balls off if he ever stepped out on me. You're working at the diner, right?"

I nodded.

"Then you've met him. Rae. He cooks for them."

"He's great!" I told her eagerly.

Suddenly the scissors were against my neck, and she was in my face. I gripped the arms of my chair, scared stiff.

"Don't get any ideas," she growled.

I just stared at her in shock.

Suddenly, she was back to normal, cutting my hair again like nothing had happened. She laughed loudly, the sound of it ringing around the salon. "You should have seen your face," she cackled.

This chick was certifiable.

"Rae will take care of you there. Just tune out his bad jokes. He thinks he's funny, but he's not."

She continued to chat away as she picked up her hair dryer and began drying my hair with a big round brush. I was a little too out of sorts to contribute much. Between her story about Daxon and Wilder and the crazy look in her eye when she threatened me with the scissors, I was just going to be quiet for now.

Miyu lifted up the bottom of my hair to dry it and then abruptly dropped her hair dryer. I jumped at the noise

"There are bruises on your neck, like fingerprints," she said softly.

We watched each other through the reflection in the mirror. Her gaze was all too knowing. I opened my mouth to give the standard excuses I'd always given in the past when someone out in the public noticed an injury Alistair had given me. I fell...or I ran into something...or I tripped.

I caught myself just in time.

"My ex was a bad man," I said simply, and she nodded, a haunted expression on her face like she knew from experience about bad men. She squeezed my shoulder softly and then picked up the hair dryer and got back to work.

It felt freeing to say the truth for once. The feeling overwhelmed me, so much so that my eyes started to prick as this was never anything I'd spoken to anyone. Those in Alistair's pack knew what he did to me, and most ignored it. Except for Nelly, and in a way, Miyu reminded me of her.

"Tada!" Miyu announced, and I realized I'd been sitting there, lost in my head for quite some time because my hair was done. I looked up.

All I could do was gape at my reflection. My hair was cut in face-framing layers. With the dead ends removed, my hair seemed shinier, brighter...almost unreal. It was still long, hanging more than halfway down my back, but it had volume and shape now.

"You look good," Miyu announced, and I just nodded, still stunned at the transformation. It was amazing the effect a haircut could have, even on the way your face looked. I swore my eyes even seemed brighter and livelier.

"Thank you," I said, emotion leaking into my words. I wiped at my eyes, embarrassed, but Miyu mercifully didn't comment on my tears.

She took off my cape, and I stood up, fumbling for the little purse I'd brought with me. "How much do I owe you?" I asked in a stilted voice, unable to look her in the eye.

"This one's on the house," she replied firmly.

I dragged my gaze to hers in shock. "I can pay you," I told her, those irritating tears coming back full force.

"Consider this my contribution to your new start. We all need one sometimes."

My heart melted as I stood there, and I just nodded gratefully.

"Thank you," I whispered.

"And besides, with how good you look, you're like free advertising as you walk around town. Just tell everyone who did your hair. Ira across town is always trying to poach my clients, and this will drive her nuts."

I giggled and then nodded. "I'll tell everyone you're a master at your craft."

She winked at me. "I'm counting on it."

I said my goodbyes and walked out of the salon, feeling somehow a thousand pounds lighter than when I'd gone in.

~

I was back at work, my beautiful new hair pulled back in a ponytail unfortunately, so that I didn't drag it through everyone's food. There had been no sign of

Wilder, thank goodness, and the place was so busy, I didn't have time to think about anything else.

The bell on the door chimed, signaling that a new customer had just come in, but I didn't bother looking up until I noticed that the chatter in the restaurant had suddenly dimmed.

Looking around confused, I stiffened when I saw that Daxon was standing by the door with a sexy smirk on his face.

I momentarily lost the ability to think as I stared at him.

He was so fucking beautiful.

Daxon strolled right towards me without even looking at Eve, who'd just rushed up to seat him. He settled himself down in the chair at the counter, right by where I'd been frantically rolling silverware since we were about to run out.

"Hi, sweetheart," he drawled, his use of sweetheart having a far different effect on me than Wilder's had.

"H-hi," I stuttered nervously, my fingers fumbling with a spoon. He caught it right before it dropped to the floor.

"Can I get you anything?" I asked, looking anywhere but his face, since it seemed to have the ability to make me stupid.

"Dinner," he responded with a low laugh that sent goosebumps across my skin.

My gaze snapped to him, confused, and I blushed at the way he looked like he wanted to devour me. "Here's a menu?" I said haltingly as I tried to hand him one.

He threw his head back in response, a rich, throaty laugh coming out of him that had the unfortunate effect of making me want to jump him. No one was allowed to sound that sexy laughing. Especially when they looked like him. I found myself wondering what else I could say to elicit that sound over and over again.

"Dinner with you, tonight after your shift," he clarified.

The butterflies I'd been feeling since he'd walked into the diner turned into bees as I stared at him uncomprehendingly. There was no way that this guy was asking me out. There was a certain way that the world worked, and it never changed. Men like him didn't end up with girls like me. It was just how it was.

Especially broken girls like me who had nothing left to offer someone.

I closed my eyes thinking this must be some kind of joke.

"This isn't funny," I whispered.

His eyes widened in confusion at the tears threaded through my words.

"I don't know what you mean, Rune." His gold eyes stared at me earnestly, dancing all over my face like they had when I'd first met him. There was something in his gaze... It almost looked like awe.

I'd once imagined what it would be like for my fated mate to look at me like that. And then I'd realized a look like that was just a lie. Alistair had looked at me like that.

Right before he held me down, raped me, and then told me I'd never get the chance to meet my wolf.

The thing about men who got that look in their eye, is that they wanted to own you. And once they did, they didn't know how to do it without breaking you.

"I can't do dinner," I told him abruptly, not caring if he was joking or not, but knowing I didn't want anything to do with it. Besides the fact that I had enough emotional baggage to bury someone, I wasn't about to start getting in the same situation I'd just gotten away from. And there was the fact that after meeting his crazy ex, or maybe ex, and hearing the story from Miyu today, that wasn't a situation I wanted anything to do with.

His looks may temporarily stop my heart every time I saw him, but they weren't worth the pain of a broken heart.

And that's all a face like his could give a girl.

"Why not?" he asked as he got out of his chair and began following me as I walked back to the bar to pick up some drinks for a few of my tables.

"I just don't want to," I told him stiffly, grabbing the drinks and hoping that he would get the hint that I was done with the conversation.

I felt his touch on my arm, and I flinched, almost dropping the tray of drinks. I'd felt literal shocks at his touch.

The problem was I couldn't tell if they were good or bad.

"Just one dinner and then you can never talk to me again." I swung around to look at him, not surprised by the smug expression on his face like he knew that I'd never be able to stop at just one dinner.

"This is just a brief stop in my life. As soon as I get that car fixed, I'm done. I don't have time for distractions like you," I hissed, hating the way his eyes hardened at my words.

Hurt flashed through his gaze, and then he nodded, his face going blank in a way that made my heart ache.

"See you around, Rune," he said quietly before leaving. I could feel everyone's gaze on me as he walked out... including Wilder's, who'd just walked in.

Needing a break, I grabbed the stock list from behind the counter and headed to the back where all the liquor and beer were kept to take inventory and give myself a break from all the eyes.

I no sooner had stepped inside the room when the door suddenly slammed open behind me and Wilder was there, his chest heaving as he pushed me against the wall.

"W-Wilder—" I stuttered, fear and something else I didn't want to name shooting through my insides.

"Why was he talking to you?" he growled, and I swear his green eyes sparked as he stared at me furiously.

"Daxon?" I asked, confused. His face tightened when I said Daxon's name, as if it was literally painful for him to even hear his name.

Without warning, his mouth claimed mine. The hard press of his lips forced my mouth open. I moaned when his tongue swept in, the taste of chocolate and mint mixed with the heady tang of desire overwhelming all my senses.

I'd never imagined a kiss like this... I'd never have been able to comprehend how the bold sweep of his tongue would feel as it teased my own. It was as if he were pulling the very breath from my body till it forced me to breathe in his own air to live. His shadow of a beard scraped against the delicate skin of my cheeks and chin, and I welcomed the pain and the pleasure it brought. If it hadn't been for the shelf behind me and the hard press of his body against mine, I would have fallen. He was consuming me like he needed me to breathe...to live.

I couldn't get enough of the feel of him. All rational thought left my head. All I could think was more. More of his touch, more of his kiss...more of him.

His tongue licked my lips and something felt like it was going to burst out of my chest, like it needed to be as close to Wilder as possible.

He pressed harder against me, and a handle of vodka clattered to the floor, bringing us both crashing back to reality.

Wilder ripped his lips away from mine as if the act physically hurt him and all but roared a loud "Fuck" that echoed through the small stock room.

And then he was gone, the door slamming behind him and sending another bottle to the floor that this time shattered.

I gripped my chest, trying to quell the ache inside of me.

I wanted to scream...or cry. I couldn't decide which one.

All I could think in that moment though was when Wilder's lips had been against mine, I hadn't thought of Alistair, not once.

And I hated that it felt like betrayal.

～

I needed to run. The urge was constant. The need bordered on pain as I paced my room, trying to walk the feeling away. I tried to do crunches...and then lunges. Nothing worked. If I didn't get out of here...if I didn't feel the wind whipping across my face as I pushed myself, I was going to go crazy.

Finally, I couldn't control myself any longer, and even though I knew the danger, I found myself on the sidewalk, running as fast as I was able, smiling as I breathed in the fresh air that somehow smelled of flowers and sunshine...if that was even possible.

I wound my way through the town, finally getting to the dirt path that led to the river. *I would just stay away from the woods, much farther away than yesterday*, I told myself. I ran, faster and faster, until the world seemed to be a blur around me. All I could think of was that I needed to be free. I needed to move and feel that burn in my lungs that meant I was still alive...that I was still here.

I needed to run until I couldn't remember what Wilder tasted like.

It came out of nowhere then, a sharp growl was all I

heard before immense pressure, followed by a sharp bite of pain ripping through my thigh. The pressure abruptly released, and I fell to the ground, hot tears streaming down my face as something large and menacing hovered over me. I opened my mouth to scream, sure that this was the end. Right as the creature opened its mouth, something barreled into it, pushing it away from me. Sitting up and trying to get away as pain surged through me, I came to an abrupt halt as a raven colored wolf attacked the thing in front of me. It sank its jaw into the beast's jugular as its growls slashed through the air around us. The creature let out a rage filled cry and somehow managed to tear itself away from the wolf, blood spattering the ground around it. It burst away before I could get a good look at it.

The wolf took a few steps after it, growling softly.

As I watched, its whole body began to quiver, and faster than a blink, where there had just been a wolf...there was now a man.

Everything went black after that, the mixture of blood loss and shock too much for my body to stand.

*S*oft voices around me. A whisper of a caress across my face. Consciousness came slowly back to me. I dragged my eyes open, everything around me hazy and out of focus.

"Rune," a familiar voice called.

It took me a second to realize who it was. All I saw was gold at first. And then things sharpened until Daxon came into view, leaning over me, a look of concern written all over his perfect face.

I blinked a few times slowly. "What happened?" I asked in a scratchy voice as I just stared at him, confused.

"You were running, and you just tripped and hit your head. Someone found you on the trail by the river," he answered in that smooth voice of his.

I blinked for a few times, trying to understand why that didn't sound right. What had I been doing?

It all hit me at once. The images tumbled through my mind until I felt weighed down, panicky...like I couldn't breathe.

I struggled to sit up, my hand automatically going to my

thigh where I knew I'd feel blood. I saw Marcus standing a few feet away, looking at me with uncertainty.

I stopped for a second, shaking my head as I kept trying to get my wits back. I stared at my leg unblinkingly, not understanding why my leg was perfectly fine. I was wearing my black leggings... I mean, they looked like my black leggings. And there wasn't a rip or a tear in them. There wasn't any blood stain either. I timidly touched the area where I swore the beast's teeth had ripped into my skin. No pain. No wound. Nothing.

"Rune?" Daxon questioned, and I drew my gaze away from leg.

"I was running, and then there was some kind of beast. It came at me out of nowhere," I whispered haltingly, again tracing the area on my leg that should have been missing a chunk. "It bit me. I swear it did. And I thought...I thought I was going to die. And then a wolf. It attacked the creature. It wounded it and saved me. And then the thing ran away." A hiccupped sob came out of me as I relived the moment, as clear as if I was watching it happen right then. "And then the wolf, it changed into a man. Right in front of me. It was a shifter."

I stared at Daxon, looking for any sign of recognition at the term shifter. Any sign at all that he believed me. His gaze was unreadable. He still had that same concerned expression on his face.

"Baby, none of that happened. You didn't have a wound. You must have dreamed that after you hit your head."

I shook my head viciously. "No, I swear it happened. I swear."

"Then where's your wound? Marcus didn't see anyone else on the trail when he found you," he told me gently, his hand touching my face softly, driving me to distraction.

"It's true. There was no one else there," Marcus said quietly.

"I..." My response faded away. I didn't have an answer. As a latent wolf, I didn't have supernatural healing abilities or anything else special enough to warrant the kind of healing that would've had to take place for there to be no sign of a wound like that.

I shivered, folding my arms around myself, fear dripping down my insides. Was I going crazy? Was that what was happening here? Because I didn't understand how I could have imagined something like that. Had everything that had happened finally made me crack?

Another sob came out of me, and then I was in Daxon's arms. And I suddenly felt warm...and safe. I could feel the heat of skin through his shirt. The steady thump of his heartbeat soothed my fractured nerves. I memorized the way his arms felt wrapped around me. I inhaled his scent of sandalwood and lemon. For a moment, it seemed as though I'd stumbled into heaven.

If heaven accepted crazy people.

I finally, reluctantly pushed away from him. For a second, I thought I saw guilt in those golden eyes of his, but he blinked and whatever I'd seen was gone.

I shakily pushed my hair out of my face, a tremble sounding through my laugh. "I must have hit my head pretty hard," I murmured.

He hummed, not really agreeing or disagreeing with me.

"Thank you, Marcus," I whispered as I struggled to stand up then. He just nodded in response.

"Hey, take as much time as you need," Daxon said anxiously as he put out a hand to help.

I stood there unsteadily, overwhelmingly tired. I was overcome with emotion. Was I really losing my mind?

I couldn't think of another explanation.

"I just need to get back to the inn and sleep," I told Daxon wearily.

"I've got my bike outside," Marcus offered.

A low, threatening growl came out of Daxon's throat, and Marcus' eyes widened. He held up his hands and took a step backwards. "Just kidding," he said quickly.

The men here sure were growly, I thought idly, my mind too full to really think too much on it.

"I'll get you home. We're just down the street," said Daxon firmly. Suddenly, I found myself swooped up into his arms, my body humming at his proximity and that scent of his.

"What are you doing?" I asked, too tired to assert my female independence and all the other things I should be saying right now. I laid my head down on his shoulder, not really caring where we were going as long as I found a bed soon.

"I don't trust you'd be able to hold on if I took my bike, so we're walking there," Daxon explained, but I was already on my way to dreamland.

"Hey, man, I didn't know," I thought I heard Marcus say. But his words didn't make sense.

Daxon's smooth walk combined with his steady heartbeat soothed me into a sort of in between dreamland. I was barely aware of us making it to the inn, or that Daxon took me into my room and laid me down on my bed.

I was barely aware of his lips that brushed against my forehead and the strange look in his gaze as he stared down at me or his touch as he brushed a strand of hair from my face.

I was barely aware of anything.

But that night, I dreamed.

"*It's going to be perfect," my mother said brightly as she zipped up the back of my dress. I touched the lace, a little in awe. The dress was gorgeous. The second I'd seen it in the store window, I knew it would be perfect for tonight. And even though it was way beyond our budget, my mother had agreed. It wasn't every day you were presented to your fated mate.*

"Tonight will be the best night of your life," she promised me.

I just wondered why her eyes said something else. Threads of trepidation began to weave their way through me. Who was I kidding... They'd been building the second I'd seen Alistair at that pack dinner.

At eighteen, you're brought to your first pack dinner. It's supposed to be the moment when you're accepted and become a member of the pack family. I'd been excited...and terrified to go. Mother was an omega, the weakest member of the pack, and she didn't go to many pack events or talk very much—if at all— about the ones she did attend. She'd never said anything outright bad about the pack, but she always came home...defeated. I wasn't sure if that was the right description. It was an odd, uncomfortable feeling.

But any uncomfortableness had disappeared when I'd walked into the hall and felt it, that pull, like a string was snapping into place, propelling me into the room as if I had no control. Our eyes had met, and that had been it.

I'd loved him the moment I saw him, convinced that the moon goddess must have blessed me to give me someone like him.

Mother smiled at me again, and I took a deep breath, drawing strength from her sweet smile. I trusted my mother with every- thing in me. If she told me everything was going to be great, I could believe her.

Straightening my shoulders, I smoothed out my dress one

more time. The dress was a navy-blue color with a black lace overlay. It was mermaid style, perfectly form-fitting until it flared out at the bottom. It had a sweetheart neckline that displayed my mother's necklace perfectly. I'd been shocked when she'd presented it as one of my eighteenth birthday presents. I'd loved that necklace since I'd found it in her bedside table. And even though she never wore it, always telling me it was too special to wear all the time, as a child, I'd often peeked looks at it whenever I was in her room.

Now that I was wearing it, I had trouble not touching it constantly, afraid that it would fall off and get lost. My mother had tears in her eyes when she gave it to me. It was the most special thing I'd ever owned.

"Ready to go?" she asked, shaking me out of my thoughts. I looked at her face one more time, looking for the reassurance I, at eighteen, still desperately needed.

"He's your true mate," she whispered. "It will be just like all the stories we've always talked about."

"Let's do this," I answered, giddy anticipation pushing away the fear...at least a little.

There was a car waiting outside of our apartment. I wouldn't expect less since my true mate happened to be the next alpha, something I could barely comprehend. I didn't know yet where I would fall in the pack as far as dominance went, but since my mother was an omega...chances were I wasn't going to blow anyone away.

I took another deep breath, my heart dropping a bit when I saw that Alistair wasn't inside the car. I slid into the cool leather interior, rubbing my arms, suddenly chilled.

The ride was silent. The driver didn't put down the privacy screen at all, and my mother was oddly quiet and tense the entire time. The lights of the city passed by, but I didn't stare at them with the same avid fascination as I usually did. It felt like I was *on the edge of a precipice right now...my whole life about to change.*

And I was terrified.

The car finally came to a stop, and my door was opened by the driver, who once again, didn't say anything. I moved to slide out of the car, but I was stopped by my mother clenching my arm tightly.

"You know I love you very much, darling. Right?" she asked, again with that falsely bright voice.

"Of course," I whispered back to her. "And I you." It was how we always responded to that question.

She let me go, almost reluctantly, and then I walked to my future.

The meeting hall was packed. I wasn't sure if the enormous numbers were usual, or if it was because the alpha heir apparently had found his mate, but this many people in one room was making my skin crawl.

I'd never been one for crowds, preferring the outdoors over anything, much to my mother's chagrin. I stiffened as a few people pushed past me to get into the room, and I was almost knocked over.

But there could have been a thousand people in the room and I still wouldn't have had trouble finding him.

Alistair.

My soul gave a sigh of relief as soon as I spotted him, lounging in a chair as he entertained his adoring subjects. The group gathered around him couldn't take their eyes off him.

I didn't blame them. I couldn't take my eyes off of him either.

It was as if a spotlight was shining on him, the way the light highlighted the top of his head, giving him a halo effect and adding an extra shine to his perfect sable hair that he didn't need. He threw back his head and laughed at something the man next to him said, and I swore the sound wove its way around my heart and through my veins, running through my body and changing me into something I didn't recognize.

His green eyes, the color of spring, gazed at me then. They held me frozen in place the moment they locked on me. He smiled, his full lips showcasing a row of brilliant white teeth. Alistair stood up and strode towards me, single-minded in purpose, waving off anyone who tried to speak to him.

"Hi," I whispered when he finally stood there in front of me.

He reached out a hand and touched my cheek, and I couldn't help but lean into the feel of him, my eyes closing as I soaked in the sensation of feeling my mate's touch for the first time.

"Mine," he growled suddenly, the low purr echoing through my insides.

"Yours," I agreed shyly, and he grinned, his smile becoming my new favorite thing in the world.

I knew my world would always revolve around him from that moment on. He was the sun that I was meant to worship all my life.

"You're stunning," he told me, as if he couldn't believe his good fortune in having me there in front of him. Alistair took my hand and began to lead me towards the far side of the room where his father, the alpha, and his mother were waiting.

I looked back to find my own mother, but she'd disappeared somewhere in the crowd. I frowned, wondering if I should try to find her for this part.

"We'll get this over with quickly," Alistair told me, shooting me another grin and pulling me forward faster.

"This part" was one of the things I'd been dreading. A blood test that would determine my lineage and ensure there weren't any defects that would cause issues in the alpha's line. It wasn't supposed to be a big deal, a precaution taken because of an alpha's mate a great distance in the past who had turned out to have schizophrenia. It had come on a year after the marriage, and *the woman had almost ended the alpha bloodline forever during a hallucination.*

My mother had explained all of this and assured me there wasn't anything I needed to be worried about. Our blood was pure.

My stomach was still in knots thinking about it.

The alpha stared at me coldly, disapproval written across his features in a way that I hadn't expected. His features were Alistair in thirty years, and I shivered under his handsome, disdainful stare, trying not to visibly wilt under his attention.

Alistair's mother, Queen Lydia, was only marginally better. She gave me a small nod, lightly touching my hand as if it was cursed when I was introduced to her. I'd of course seen them from afar at various times growing up, but this was the first time I officially met them both. They wouldn't be the warmest of in-laws that was for sure. But having Alistair would make up for that.

The alpha and the queen had little to say to me, and having my blood drawn in front of the three of them in the small room behind the meeting hall was incredibly uncomfortable. The doctor gave me a reassuring smile after he was finished and then scurried out of the room to test it.

Alistair guided me to a chair, and we settled in for the short wait.

Ten minutes passed. Then twenty.

The alpha growled in frustration as he paced in front of the fire. "What the hell is taking so long?" he barked as if the rest of us somehow were responsible for the doctor's tardiness.

A feeling of dread was settling over my skin the longer I sat there. I needed my mother. Alistair's face was now riddled with worry, and he'd let go of my hand as if he already knew something was wrong with me. Everyone in the room knew the doctor's absence was not a good thing.

The door finally opened and the doctor peeked his head in, his face completely blank.

"Alpha...sir," he said, nodding at the alpha and Alistair. "Could I speak to you privately?"

My insides dropped at the doctor's somber tone. There couldn't be anything wrong with me, right?

Alistair and the alpha disappeared from the room without a look back. I fiddled with the fabric on my dress nervously, flicking off invisible pieces of lint. I could feel the disapproving gaze of the queen heavy on the top of my head, and I intentionally kept staring at my lap.

The time that passed was excruciating. A loud bang followed by a heavy thump suddenly ricocheted through the room, the sound coming from behind the door that Alistair and the alpha had disappeared behind. I looked at the queen questioningly, but she just sat there stiffly, no concern in her features.

I went back to studying my lap, my nerves on high alert. The door finally opened, and Alistair and the alpha prowled back in.

The doctor didn't follow them.

I tried to look at Alistair for clues, but he wouldn't meet my gaze. His entire frame was stiff and unwelcoming. The dread in my stomach was in full force now, and I was sure that I was going to throw up at any moment.

The alpha muttered something to Alistair and prodded him in the back. Alistair stiffened somehow even more, and then he finally looked at me.

The words he uttered after that became etched into my soul, carved so deep, there would never be a way to forget...or recover.

"Rune Celeste Esmeray, I hereby reject you as my mate and sever our bond. From this time forward, you are nothing to me. I swear this under the moon goddess."

Alistair's words were cold and firm, and they sliced through me like glass.

I sank to my knees, the ache in my chest so terrible, it felt like I was dying. I clenched the fabric of my dress, trying to hold myself together. Something shattered inside of me. It took me a moment to realize it was my heart.

I was destroyed, ravaged...ruined.

"You are a blight to this pack. You will serve in my son's household so a close eye can be kept on you and no further shame brought upon your family or our kind," the alpha said then.

His words didn't register though. I was on the floor, my soul leaking out from the wound spreading in my chest.

I wished for death as I lay there, and they left me like that, slamming the door behind me as they all left the room.

While I lay there, my shame was announced to the crowded room, and my mother left me willingly, telling the alpha she never wanted to see me again.

I was alone, a bitter and terrible future laid out for me that I'd never dreamed I would see.

And even after all that was done to me in the many days that followed...

I still loved him.

~

Sweat dripped down my spine as I emerged from my nightmare. I did my best to not think of that day, the day that had changed the course of my whole life. Evidently, my dreams hadn't gotten the memo.

I threw the covers off, desperate to get some air. I tried to take deep, soothing breaths and calm my racing heart. The urge to tear at my skin was always present when I thought about that day. I raced to the window and threw it open, sucking in big gulps of the fresh night air outside.

My heartbeat finally slowed down enough for me to think clearly.

"I'm here. That's over. I escaped. I'm free," I whispered to myself, a mantra I had to tell myself daily.

Leaning on the windowsill, I put my face on my hands, my body beginning to shake. Sometimes, it felt like I'd never truly be free. Lifting my head up, I stared at the moon, its pale light somehow lighting up the whole black sky. And for the first time in a very long time, I pleaded to the moon goddess, asking for relief from the pain I could never seem to get rid of.

She didn't answer me.

But I hadn't expected her to.

She never had before.

∼

*N*eedless to say, when I went to work the next day, I was not in a good mood. And even though I tried to do all the things that I knew would help with tips, I was off.

Evidenced by the fact I'd just dumped a Sprite in a customer's lap.

Fuck.

I stormed to the back, leaving Eve to give the customer a towel. I didn't have it in me to give them the necessary niceties my accident would require. I'd just have to give Eve any tip they left, not that I expected that to happen.

In the back, I started to fold silverware, hoping that the rest of my tables could survive without me for a few minutes while I got my head on straight.

But doing any task seemed to be impossible for me as I reached for the silverware, and instead, accidentally pushed the entire tray onto the floor, the clang of the metal against the tile reverberating loudly around me.

"Seriously?" I heard Wilder's voice snarl from behind me.

And that was it. I'd had enough.

I passed the bar, ignoring where Wilder was staring at me, and I all but ran to the hallway where I leaned against the wall and tried to get ahold of myself.

I wondered when it would ever get easier to not let the past leak into the present and try to ruin it.

"What the hell is wrong with you? I'm not paying you to stand around and take breaks whenever you want!" growled Wilder from a few feet away.

I tried to stop myself, I really did.

It just didn't work.

"Can you shut the hell up and leave me along for five fucking minutes?" I snapped at him, my entire body shaking with rage. Something inside my chest felt like it was about to leap at him, and I had to hold on to the molding on the wall behind me to keep myself in place.

Wilder just stared at me astonished for a minute as I held my breath, just knowing he was about to fire me. I mean, for someone who was supposed to be on their best behavior trying to hold onto the job they desperately needed, I was constantly toeing the line with him. And I definitely had just blown right past that line just now.

Wilder snapped into action then and before I could blink, he'd hauled me around the corner and his body was pressed against me. His mouth claimed mine in a bruising kiss filled with a thousand dark promises that I couldn't examine just then. He grasped my face with both hands as his mouth claimed me, again and again. His taste was addictive, and my tongue swirled and danced against his, just trying to get more. I grasped the thin soft material of his shirt, trying to pull him even closer to me as my moan and our combined harsh breathing echoed in the hall around us.

His hand wrapped around my throat, not too tight, just to let me know that in this moment, I belonged to him and there was nothing I could do about it.

I waited for the familiar panic to spring up inside of me that had always followed Alistair's domination of me.

But there was nothing like that. If anything, it just fanned the flames of lust threatening to break out of control all over my body. There was a building ache inside of me, and I was desperate for him to ease the pain. His lips moved from my mouth down my neck as he inched my skirt farther up until one of his hands was dancing along the line of my thong. I thrust against him, unable to do anything but follow the blind passion that had overtaken my brain.

One long finger moved beneath the elastic finally, and a high-pitched keen escaped my lips as he ran his finger along my soaking wet seam.

My entire body shivered at the sensation, my breath coming out in gasps. More, more, more, I chanted, not realizing I was saying it out loud until I felt his dark chuckle against my skin.

"I'll give you more, baby. Fuck. All I've been able to think about is this sweet pussy."

His words should have confused me, but I was beyond all rational thought as he pushed the tip of his finger inside of me, his grip against my neck holding me in place. When I didn't object, he added another finger and used them both to push into my swollen sex, curling them, rubbing unerringly over my sensitive bundle of nerves with each thrust. He let out a quiet groan as he continued to lick and kiss farther down my neck and then my chest.

His fingers pushed deeper into me, hitting another sensitive spot that sent electricity shooting through me. My body tensed, a strangled moan escaping me as my muscles clenched viciously. All of my muscles. My stomach compressed, and I let out a violent scream that he caught with his lips. I clamped my thighs together, holding him inside of me. "Ah," I gasped into his mouth, unable to form words from the unexplainable pleasure he was giving me.

And then I came.

So violent and explosive, I forgot to breathe. It felt like miniature explosions all over my body, working their way through me. Through it all, he kissed me, all-consuming kisses that made me temporarily forget my name and where I was. I gasped in air, trying to compose myself. Trying to gain control again. My orgasm slowly faded, and my thighs fell open, letting go of his hand still buried inside of me.

"Fuck," he moaned as he slid his fingers from me and sucked them clean. I watched in a daze at how he seemed to savor the taste, like it was frosting off his favorite cake.

Everything came roaring back just then—where we were, what we'd just done. I pulled my underwear back in place and yanked my skirt down, my face heating and reddening as I looked anywhere but at him.

He let go of my throat then, almost reluctantly, and his fingers trailed down my chest, eliciting a thousand more shivers with his touch. I couldn't speak, and shame coated my throat, leaving me voiceless.

"You're wild, baby," he whispered in a rough, lust-ridden voice. "I never would've thought you had it in you."

His words unfroze me then, and I darted to the side, breaking all contact, even as my body begged for more.

"I've got to get back to work," I told him in a low, ashamed whisper.

"Rune?" he asked, anger beginning to leak into his voice at my reaction.

I darted down the hall, only faltering slightly when he roared and I heard the sound of his fist hitting the wall, pieces of the drywall and plaster falling to the ground.

I didn't look back.

I threw myself back into work, knowing at the end of the day I wouldn't be able to recall who had come in or what I had served.

"You're wild, baby," was on repeat in my head for the rest of the day...and into the night, the rugged cadence of his words sending my hands into my panties as I laid restlessly in bed.

And when I fell over that cliff, pleasure surging up my spine, all I could think when I finished was that I deserved everything bad that had ever happened to me.

"I said I wanted cheese fries, and these are not it."
The woman in the booth at the diner pushed her plate of food across the table back at me. "If you have trouble taking orders, maybe I ought to talk to your boss." She reclined in her seat, her smug face infuriating me. Her two friends, also in the booth, were giggling, obviously delighting in the fact they were making my life hell.

I clenched my teeth and smiled because as they say, the customer is always right. But really, whoever made up that crap had obviously never worked in the service industry.

"Ma'am, this is your third meal you'll be sending back. This is what you ordered," I explained, glancing over to her second round of free beer on the table, untouched. "Is there something wrong with the food?"

I really didn't want to face Rae again, who was already fuming with the first two returned dishes he had to remake.

And I knew I hadn't gotten those orders wrong.

She narrowed her eyes, looking ready to spit fire in my direction. "Do you get off on going after men that belong to someone else?" she suddenly asked.

And there it was, the truth of why these ladies were acting like this. A scorching embarrassment rose up over my neck and across my cheeks. Had these girls seen Wilder join me in the hallway the other day...or the stockroom?

They obviously were friends with Arcadia, because who else would care who I had been with? My pulse spiked at the thought, filling me with trepidation.

Just then, the bell to the front door dinged, and from the corner of my eye, I saw Daxon walk in. My whole body buzzed because just like Wilder, Daxon affected me in ways I didn't understand. I often found myself tripping and forgetting how to speak in his presence. I might as well be back in high school.

The brunette at the table watched him, then looked at me, her upper lip curling into a snarl. "See even now, you can't help yourself. I can see the desperation on your face when you look at him."

Okay. Maybe she wasn't talking about Wilder after all... thank the moon goddess. I didn't want to think there'd been an audience for what I'd allowed to happen a few days ago.

I just wanted to forget it, period.

But each time I had to go take stock...or walk down that hallway, which still displayed the hole Wilder had put in it, all I could picture was Wilder's lips on mine. The incredible feel of his body. The pleasure he'd given me.

My body had betrayed me. I was the problem. I only knew how to be attracted to the bad guys.

"Hello, are you daydreaming about giving him a blowjob?" the brunette barked loud enough for everyone in the diner to hear.

I resisted the urge to look around and see if Daxon heard. Based on her anger, I could only imagine she had been one of his flings when he'd split up with Arcadia...

which explained the bitterness. I would have been bitter too.

But why on Earth was she trying to take it out on me right now?

"So, just to confirm, you want different cheese fries. But your untouched burger is fine?" I hissed, ignoring her comment.

She made a grunting noise at me, and I'd had enough. I grabbed her plate and marched across the room, noting Daxon had taken a seat at the last booth near the bar area.

Eve took the plate from me when I reached the counter. "Here, let me take care of this. I'm so sick of those bitches. I'm going to shove a fucking fork right up her nose, then scramble her tiny brain."

I laughed, loving how creative she was in her torture.

"Go and serve Daxon. You should have seen the way he stared at you as he walked in."

"Really? No, he wasn't." My cheeks burned.

She gave my arm a light squeeze. "Go and make the bitches squirm in their seat."

When she shoved past the kitchen door, I immediately heard Rae's raised voice. I licked my lips and grabbed a menu, scuttling away quickly so Rae couldn't yell at me. I rounded the counter, making my way over to Daxon.

Why in the world was I sweating so much? The last time I saw him, I'd just woken up from having evidently collapsed during my run. I shook my head a bit, the memory of that wolf attack...that had apparently never happened...so vivid in my brain.

I wasn't sure what was going on with me lately, but as the day passed, my resolve only grew that I hadn't imagined everything. I had been attacked.

Daxon sat with his back to me, and I stepped up to the

table, gaining his attention. He greeted me with a warm smile, and my heart fluttered. I'd seen his ferocity when he fought Wilder in the inn, yet in my presence, he was the complete opposite, appearing anything but hostile.

"What would you like to order?" My voice came out almost as a squeak, and I cleared my throat, wishing I could just act normal around him.

His golden, hazel eyes gleamed against the sunlight pouring in from the window, his skin a beautifully tanned shade, and I could easily picture him as one of those powerful lumberjacks coming in after a day's work. He sure had the body for it.

"The diner's quiet. Take a seat with me," he suggested, his voice husky. He leaned back, arms stretched out across the back of the booth on either side of him, and I noticed he couldn't go long without taking his gaze off me.

I hesitated at first, pretty sure I knew where this invite was headed. But what was the harm in entertaining his offer to join him for a chat? The only customers left were an older couple chatting over a cold bowl of wedges for the past hour and the bitch clan. If I could avoid them, I'd do it in a heartbeat.

"Sure, I can spare a few minutes."

DAXON

Fuck.

I wanted Rune more than I'd wanted anyone in my whole fucking life. And it had nothing and everything to do with that prick, Wilder staring at her like he'd already claimed her the other night at The Lair Inn.

And the little dove in front of me had no clue he was even watching her.

Now, she shuffled into the booth seat across from me, trying to put on a brave face, even as nerves danced behind her eyes. She kept fiddling with the menu she still hadn't given me. She was...refreshing...intriguing? I couldn't keep my mind off of her, and I should have known from the moment I met her at Dentworks I wouldn't be able to stay away.

Something about her made me feel alive, and it had been too long since someone had been able to wake me this way. She'd been on my mind daily, and not even sleep steered her away, as she filled my dreams.

"I know what you want to talk to me about," she said.

"Yeah, and what's that?" I couldn't resist taunting her, my lips quirking into a grin.

She seemed a bit dazed when I smiled, and it only made my lips widen more, wanting to elicit any kind of reaction from her.

I had told myself to keep my distance and let her be. That shit went out the window the moment I stepped in the diner, spotting her delicate curved body and long blonde hair I wanted to wrap around my hands and use to hold her against me.

She watched me with her unnerving blue gaze, and it twisted my insides up even more.

I had the urge to scoot closer. It was painful to remain so far from her. She didn't seem the kind to be pushed though, so I held myself back, reminding myself that I needed to wait until she was ready.

"I know you want to invite me out for dinner again," she answered, rather proud of herself. I stiffened in my pants, that cute little temptress smile of hers sure to fill my thoughts for a while.

"You seem pretty sure of yourself. What if you're wrong?"

She leaned back, hugging the menu to her chest. Was there such a thing as being envious of a piece of cardboard?

"I'm certain of it," she announced, trying to sound confident. I smirked again. She might not realize it now, but she wanted exactly what I did.

I played along with her game. Everything from the way she looked at me, the tone of her voice, and how easily she'd accepted my invitation to sit down in the middle of her shift telling me she enjoyed herself.

"Are you going to enlighten me, sweetheart?"

She drew her bottom lip between her teeth, gently gnawing on it, and I caught her hitched breaths.

"Yes," she finally said.

"Yes?" I replied, arching a brow.

"Fine, if you insist, I'll go to dinner with you."

The moment the delicious words left her sweet mouth, a shattering shriek broke through our perfect moment. I twisted my head around to see Eve dumping a plate of food onto a brunette's lap. I groaned internally, recognizing her, on purpose not remembering her name as I'd shut it out long ago. She'd been a weakness that I allowed into my life when I was at my lowest point, a time when I accepted any woman to forget my shitty life. It had been a while ago, but her face still filled me with regret.

"Oh shit," Rune murmured, scrambling to get out of the booth. "Here's the menu." She practically threw it into my hands, her face blanching at the sight as she rushed toward the chaos.

Before she got too far, I grabbed her wrist, drawing her attention to me. "I'll be at the inn at eight tonight to pick you up."

Gorgeous excitement flared over her expression, and she nodded before darting over to the commotion.

In truth, my intention had been to ask her how she was doing since the other day...but going out on a date with her was way better.

RUNE

"Do you like Creole food?" Daxon asked me as he pushed open the door to a restaurant that had been tucked away in a small alleyway. I would never have thought to come down this way, but once I was inside, the food smelled heavenly. Strong aromas of roasted meat and fragrant spices burst over my senses, while bluegrass music played overhead.

"I like all food," I told him with a wink. "It smells incredible in here." I scanned the large room that had been deceivingly small from the outside. The walls were adorned with corrugated metal, each one painted with colorful murals of men out in small fishing boats, another of the landscape, and the wall above the open kitchen had a huge red lobster. Industrial, bowl shaped lights hung across the room, lighting up the long wooden tables and benches. And suddenly, my nerves melted away that we'd be going to a stuffy restaurant with everything perfectly in place.

"Hope this is suitable?" Daxon stepped inside and paused alongside me, looking at me for a response. He looked so flipping hot tonight.

"Are you kidding? This looks so amazing. I've never been to a place like this."

Daxon's smile was contagious. His happiness somehow made me giddy. I didn't know what to make of that.

Before long, we were seated at the end of a long table. Behind us, several groups of people entered the restaurant. I glanced down at the menu on our table, at the array of dishes, until my attention landed on the words *raw steak*. I kept reading the line over a few times, certain I was reading it wrong. That had to be a misprint, as no one would order a completely raw steak.

"You look beautiful," Daxon said to me, distracting me from my confusion, and I lifted my gaze to meet his. I stood no chance of holding back the smile spreading my lips as excited shivers danced down my arms. I'd purposefully gone out shopping for something to wear, and the moment I found the sky-blue strapless summer dress and silver sandals, I knew I'd found my outfit. Not too dressy, but not casual either, seeing I had no clue where we were going. Looking around, I was pleased to see that I fit in perfectly with everyone else.

"Thanks. And you shaved," I pointed out, coaxing a small laugh out of him as I tried to turn attention away from me. I felt uncomfortable in all honesty, because I didn't remember the last time anyone had told me I was beautiful.

Daxon rubbed his jawline, the shadow of growth gone, then pushed the messy loose strands of golden hair out of his eyes. His eyes still got me... They were like the rising sun, and when he peered back at me, the jitters in my stomach returned. The ones that told me he was too good for me but I couldn't help but want him just the same.

"I try to make an effort sometimes," he murmured. "Seeing as this is your first time here, how do you feel about me surprising you with ordering a few dishes for us to share?"

I nodded instantly because half the dishes listed on the menu were unrecognizable to me. He got up and sauntered over to the kitchen area. My gaze drank all of him in, from the blue jeans that curved around his firm ass to his broad shoulders in the white button-up shirt. It wasn't tight, but hugged him enough that you could easily make out his firm muscles underneath. From the moment he'd picked me up from the inn, I'd been sneaking peeks at him, unable to calm my heart or breathing.

Just calm down. It's just a distraction, remember.

Right, a distraction.

Since finishing my shift at the diner today, I'd felt like I was walking on clouds. I told myself multiple times to have no expectations...that I should even expect disappointment.

But no matter what I'd said, those words evaporated the moment I laid eyes on Daxon, dressed up and waiting for me.

At the other end of our long table, an older couple shared a large plate spilling over with seafood. They ate and chatted while admiring each other. Too adorable. A rush of sadness hit me. I'd once thought that would be me.

Daxon returned, carrying a hurricane glass with a mango-colored drink. He set it in front of me, and I inhaled the fruity smell.

"Piña colada with a twist."

I took a sip, instantly taken by the fruity sweetness. "It's really good."

He sat across from me and took a sip from his bottle of beer.

"So, do you come here often?" I asked lamely.

The corner of his mouth curled upward. "The food here is incredible, and we don't have a large selection in town. Figured Italian and Chinese you could have anywhere, and you wouldn't want diner food, so Creole it was. Plus, I wanted to see your reaction when you tasted some of these dishes. I fell in love with it the first time I came here."

I blushed slightly, loving the fact he had put thought into why he'd brought me here. "I'll try anything at least once."

"Just a warning...my appetite is ferocious and I ordered a lot." He set his beer down and leaned forward against the table. "I hope you can keep up."

I burst out laughing. "Have you seen the size of me compared to you? But I'll give it a try."

When he laughed, I was lost to the sound, admiring the way the creases around his mouth deepened, how his eyes almost closed. I needed to pinch myself to make sure I was really on a date with this man.

Not at date...a distraction.

I was a horrible liar, even to myself.

"I meant to ask you earlier how you're feeling after the fall?" He stared at me so intently, I almost forgot what he asked. How was Daxon still single?

Then his question repeated in my mind. The fall... I wasn't sure that was what I called it, but how did I argue a point when I had no evidence of the bite?

"I'm better," I answered. "Though I keep wondering if I'm going crazy with what I imagined I saw." Instinctively, I reached down to touch my leg, still half expecting to feel the bite. But the skin was smooth, not a bump or scratch. "You must be thinking I'm crazy. A wolf turning into a man..."

Daxon looked at me without judgment, and I had to remind myself not to push it. While I might have grown up around wolves, humans had no clue we existed, and he would think I was an even bigger idiot if I continued to press the point.

He reached his hand across the table, and the tips of his

fingers grazed my arm. There was something so tempting about his action, so captivating as he looked at me. I'd noticed lots of pretty girls when we'd walked in, but none of them seemed to have distracted him. His touch sent a buzz right to the core of my body.

At first, I didn't react. I wasn't sure what to do. Did I take his hand? Was this moving too fast? Or was it a simple touch of reassurance? My heart beat so fast while I tried to decide what to do.

"What else do you remember before you passed out? Did you hit your head when you fell?"

I shook my head and decided this wasn't a topic I wanted to keep discussing. "I'm sure you're right and I just dreamed it all when I passed out," was all I said, even if in my mind, I was still convinced of what I'd seen.

Maybe there was a shifter living in the woods, or a nearby pack, which scared me. I wanted no connection to them or anything that might make a link to Alistair. The man knew a lot of influential people.

The waitress arrived, and I was thrilled for the interruption. She carried a massive serving tray she lowered onto the edge of the table before placing the dishes in front of us.

My eyes bulged at the array of meals ranging from stews, to fried fish and chicken pieces, shrimp in a tomato sauce, to a steak that looked like it once belonged on a dinosaur.

Ten dishes, and I could swear that suddenly, the whole restaurant was staring at us.

"Enjoy your meal," the young woman said, only looking at Daxon, waiting for his thank you, the smile just for him. When he gave her an answering grin, she practically swooned on the spot before hurrying back toward the kitchen. There she started whispering to another waitress, both of them glancing our way.

"You have a few fans here," I said.

But Daxon just laughed and started serving me a bit from every dish to try out. He then carved into the dino steak, which was almost completely raw on the inside. Maybe the menu wasn't wrong after all. He placed a small portion on my plate and sat back and began to dig in.

"They're just young girls," he finally answered blandly, not looking their way. I glanced at them. They weren't that much younger than me.

"Try the food," he urged me eagerly as he swallowed a piece of steak.

I collected my fork and started with the fragrant stew packed with chunks of meat and shrimp as that looked delicious.

"It's gumbo. My favorite," he told me as he continued to scoop food into his mouth.

I took a mouthful, and an explosion of earthy flavors burst over my tongue. With it came a burning taste that ran down my throat as if I had swallowed a whole chili.

"Oh geez, that's spicy!" I picked up my cocktail and began to gulp it down as he laughed and poured me a glass of water.

"I probably should have mentioned the food here carries some heat."

"It's still good, but I may lose feeling in my lips." It didn't stop me from eating and trying the rest of the dishes, including the steak. Surprisingly, it was perfectly seasoned and almost melted on my tongue.

"You never told me what brought you to Amarok," he asked, then took a bite out of the garlic bread, the crunch making me reach over to take a slice as well.

"You know about my car accident." I took a bite into the

garlic treat, realizing instantly that my breath would be garlic now, but so would Daxon's.

"That's not what I mean. Why were you in this vicinity in the first place?"

I shrugged and stuffed my bread into my mouth, unsure how much I should be revealing. Alistair wasn't a topic I enjoyed talking about to anyone, let alone him. Daxon continued eating and waited patiently for me to respond, giving me enough time to decide to go with the semi-truth.

"I had a bad breakup...from a really bad guy. And I needed to get away. So I left," I said, shrugging forlornly. "I know it makes me look like a coward for running. But I don't care." I sipped from my cold, refreshing water, keeping my gaze on Daxon for his reaction. I remembered Miyu's reaction in the hair salon when she saw the bruises on the back of my neck. I didn't want that kind of pity from Daxon.

I took a deep breath, trying to push the past out of my head for at least tonight. It was always a shadow, a blemish... just waiting for me.

Daxon wiped his mouth with a napkin and sat back. "My mother once told me that no one facing darkness feels brave in the moment. It's about what we learn during the struggle that's important. I faced betrayal, and it took me a long time to walk away. What you did was a lot braver than me."

I almost wanted to laugh out loud, as he made it sound easy. "You want to know the truth?" I leaned in closer. "It took me a long time too, and it was only when a close friend pushed me that I was able to wake up and leave. And your mother sounds wise."

He half-laughed. "She was that and so much more."

With what Miyu had told me about Daxon, he would very much understand the sting of betrayal. It kind of felt liberating to talk to him about something we both shared where I didn't sense him judging me.

I grinned and kept eating. "Let's talk about something happier." I nudged him. "And you better get to work. You ordered enough to feed a small village. I don't think I've ever eaten this much food in one sitting, by the way."

"Then you are definitely going out to meals with the wrong people."

He had no idea how right he was.

"You did the right thing," he said as he drained the last bit of his beer.

"What's that?" I asked.

He glanced around for someone to order another drink, and I guessed he hadn't heard me as he was getting to his feet. Suddenly, he looked over to me, his gaze lingering on my face, an unreadable expression in his eyes.

"I'm glad you came to our town, Rune," he said sweetly. With that statement, he straightened and wove through the busy restaurant toward the bar area.

His words spun through my mind, working their way into my fractured heart. It was nice...to feel welcomed. Especially after most people, including Wilder, seemed to want me gone. Daxon and Wilder couldn't be more opposite to each other.

A female's loud cackling laughter caught my attention to a table all the way across the room near the window.

She had her back to me, dark hair falling in waves down her back, laughing uncontrollably. And across from her, my attention landed on... Sweet fuck.

It was Wilder.

Was he on a date?

I nearly choked.

As if sensing my stare, his head jerked up, our gazes

collided. His jawline tightened. I wanted to slide under the table, to vanish. Of course he and his stupid chiseled face had to be at the same restaurant as me.

I dropped my attention quickly, studying the dishes on our plates, while the food in my stomach protested. My traitorous brain began to remember the way his lips had felt across my skin.

Daxon returned just then and flopped down onto the bench across from me. "They usually aren't this bad with service. But it's a full house tonight."

I couldn't help but glance at Wilder. He was standing up, wearing a casual top and dark pants, looking way too handsome for such an asshole. The phantom memories of him kissing me, touching me...they continued to wash over me. Why was I thinking of that right now?

My stomach sank all the way to my feet, and I stiffened in my seat.

"You okay?" Daxon asked, and I broke into a laugh like somehow, he'd said something funny. Of course, I regretted it the moment the ridiculous sound leaked past my lips.

Daxon stared at me strangely, his brows rising up his forehead. I was convinced my cheeks were red as the chilis I'd been eating.

Wilder had disappeared.

I straightened in my seat, struggling to get a hold of myself as I shot what I hoped was a cute smile at Daxon. I leaned towards him, trying to distract myself from searching for Wilder in the room. I even started serving him more of the gumbo.

"Maybe the cocktail is going to my head faster than I thought. It's been a while since I drank alcohol." I cleared my throat. "So what kind of things do you like to do around here?"

He studied me, and I knew I was coming across strangely. I was pathetic. Wilder had only looked at me, and here I was self-sabotaging in front of the golden god I was lucky enough to be dining with.

"I ordered you a mojito, but if it's too much, I'll finish it off for you."

"Maybe you should."

"Speaking of things you like to do... I noticed you've been taking up running."

Before his words finished, a shadow fell over our table.

I cranked my head back, somehow not surprised to find Wilder standing there. He towered over the table, hands stiff by his side. My whole body heated up under his attention, the summer dress I wore no longer keeping me cool. It clung to my back as perspiration slid down my skin.

Wilder didn't say a word. He just stood there, watching me.

"Can we help you?" I asked just as Daxon looked ready to stand. Considering the number of people in this restaurant, it would turn to chaos if these two broke out into another testosterone battle of who was the biggest bad boy in town. There was no doubt that these two powerful men were both type A personalities.

I stiffened my shoulders, trying to look unaffected by his presence. His gaze was knowing as he stared at me though, like he knew what I tasted like.

Which he did. Fuck my life.

"Fuck off, Wilder," Daxon growled out under his breath.

The air thickened around us with tension, making even breathing a struggle. They were going to fight again, weren't they?

"What are you doing here?" Wilder snarled, ignoring Daxon, his glare slicing through me.

"Um, having dinner," I answered, holding myself tight, even as another drop of perspiration ran down my spine. "That's what happens at a restaurant."

He leaned closer to me, and Daxon had evidently had enough. He jumped to his feet, and suddenly, they were now face to face. My heart pounded at a million miles an hour, and the whole restaurant seemed to fall silent, anticipating the violence that was coming.

"Please, not here," I whispered loud enough for them to hear.

Wilder growled deep in his chest like he was an animal. "She doesn't belong here, and you know it."

"Get the fuck out of my face and get the hell out of here," Daxon answered. He leaned forward, a smug smile appearing on his handsome face. "Not this one," I thought he murmured.

Whatever he said, Daxon's words had Wilder fuming.

I was glued to my seat, my breath wedged in my chest.

"Be very careful, Daxon. This situation of ours won't last much longer." Wilder spat the words in his face before he abruptly pulled away and marched back towards his table.

The voices around us started to slowly climb back up, and Daxon took a deep inhale before taking his seat. "Sorry you had to see that. He's an asshole on the best of days."

"Yes he is," I murmured. "I'm just glad the waitress took our knives earlier," I joked, looking over to see Wilder back with his date.

Daxon laughed. "I try to draw the line at murder."

I shrugged, smiling, glad that we were somehow moving past what had just happened.

The rest of the night passed on without issue, but once we made our way back to the inn, I felt the effect of having eaten more than I should. So much for my health goals and all of that.

Daxon walked me to the entrance around the back of the inn that led right into the bar area, and I paused there. Only the light from the inn shone around us, while night swallowed everything else in sight.

"That was a great night," I said. "The best I've had in a long time. Thank you."

"I'd gladly accept the challenge to make the next one even better?" I felt his hand slide over to mine, taking hold and drawing me closer. My cheeks heated up with anticipation. I felt like a schoolgirl, waiting for her first kiss.

My gaze fell to his perfect mouth.

"So, is that a yes to a second date?" His hands found my waist, and I stumbled toward him, my hands finding his firm chest. His muscles underneath his shirt still astounded me.

"That depends," I purred, unable to believe how forward I acted. This wasn't me, but then again, I didn't know who I was anymore.

Daxon pushed his body closer to me and guided loose strands of hair behind my ear. "Depends on what?"

I tingled all over, my heartbeat soaring, unable to focus on anything but exactly where our bodies touched. Part of me screamed I shouldn't be doing this...but the other part craved so much more.

Desire coursed through me. I was well aware of where this was going, but also that Daxon hadn't once pushed me into anything I didn't want. *Let yourself go*, I told myself. I closed my eyes and lifted my chin.

His lips pressed against mine then, the touch electrifying, my body shivering in response. I inhaled his musky scent and curled my fingers in his shirt to hold him close, kissing him back as hard as I could. We spiraled into an urgent kiss I realized I was desperate for. My clit tingled with heightened sensitivity, pulsing from his incredible kiss alone as his tongue plunged into my mouth.

I whined in my throat, pulling him closer.

"If we keep going this way, I'm not letting you go all night," he promised, the arousal thick in his voice. It danced between my thighs too, drenching my underwear.

Through my foggy brain, I searched for a response, finally coming up with, "We should stop."

Words weren't needed as the disappointment washed over his face, as my own body protested from the slow build that had just begun.

"Goodnight, Rune," he said reluctantly as he leaned in and placed one final kiss on my lips before drawing back.

I instantly stepped forward as though there was an invisible pull between us that demanded I keep him close. That delicious smile crawled over his sexy mouth, and with a nod of his head, he disappeared around the corner of the inn.

Moments later, I bounced inside, excited, lost in the kiss, my lips slightly bruised from the hunger of his mouth against mine. The explosion he unleashed inside me had been powerful, life-changing.

There was just the matter of Wilder...

I blew the hair out of my face when Jim emerged from the kitchen.

"Evening," he said. "You're looking very happy."

Short of spinning on the spot, I shrugged. "I just had an incredible night."

"That's wonderful," he said as I started up the stairs to get some sleep. "We've got the Town Run coming up in just a few days by the way," he called after me. "Expect everyone to be out and about. It's one of our busiest nights."

I stopped on the stairs and looked back at him. "All right, I'll plan for that."

He nodded and headed back into the kitchen, and I raced up to my room, thinking to myself that my life just might be on the upswing.

I should have knocked on wood.

I was walking back from a luckily uneventful run when Miyu suddenly popped out from behind a door.

"Get your butt in here and get some breakfast with me," she ordered. Looking up at the sign above her, I realized I was in front of a coffee shop that I'd been meaning to try.

"I smell," I warned her.

She just laughed and pulled me inside.

It felt like I'd stepped into the past as I walked through the door. The place was eclectic, with bright red walls, black and white movie posters in frames all around the room, and a black and white checkerboard floor. Fifties style tables and chairs, of black leather and silver, were set up by the window, and I could see fancy silver coffee presses set up behind a counter laden with various assortments of baked goods.

And the smell. It was like I'd stepped right into heaven. I wasn't mad about my stronger than normal senses at the moment as I took in a deep whiff of chocolate and roasted coffee beans.

There were no other guests in here besides Miyu and me.

In short, it was perfect.

I walked up to the counter, and Miyu rang an old-fashioned silver bell that was sitting there.

A few moments passed, and then I heard the shuffling of feet as a man who looked older than Father Time himself appeared out of the back room. He had white hair...everywhere. Tufts of the stuff were even sprouting out of his ears it looked like. It was endearing and a little concerning all at the same time. Giant watery blue eyes stared at us from inch thick silver rimmed glasses. He was wearing a red apron with 'Mr. Jones' embroidered on it in a sprawling script. Underneath the apron was a well-pressed suit that wouldn't have looked out of place in one of the scenes of the movie posters he had around the room. And right on top of his head was a black bowler hat.

"Welcome, madams, to my humble abode," he said, bowing so low that I thought he was going to fall over. I giggled nervously, but Miyu just shook her head like she was used to it. "What would you like today? A latte? An Americano? An affogato? I've got anything but a PSL, as you young folk like to say," he said, sniffing disdainfully, as if the very idea of a pumpkin spice latte was offensive to him.

Before I could get a word out, he held up a hand. "You know what, I'll surprise you. No one ever dislikes a Mr. Jones' creation," he announced, shuffling towards one of the fancy presses.

"It's true, everything he makes is gold. The baked goods too. I blame him for the extra ten pounds on my ass," Miyu whispered to me. I choked on a laugh, thinking the baked goods were probably a better use of ten pounds than my Doritos had been.

I watched in awe as Mr. Jones flitted around the room, a youthful energy suddenly around him as he darted from machine to machine. His hands were moving so fast, I could barely keep track of him. This man was a coffee wizard.

Three minutes later, and two steaming cups of coffee in fancy cream and gold mugs were set on the counter. Two blueberry muffins quickly followed. My stomach growled just looking at them.

Miyu and I gave Mr. Jones some cash, which he placed in a gigantic old-fashioned register sitting on the left side of the counter. She raised an eyebrow. "This is just coffee... right?" she asked questioningly.

I'd just picked up my mug to take a sip, but her words froze me in place.

Mr. Jones looked at her sternly...and maybe a bit sheepishly too. "That was one time, young lady. And you can't argue with the results."

Miyu harrumphed impolitely, and Mr. Jones turned and shuffled away, muttering under his breath about young people in this town...or something like that.

Miyu led me to a table by the window.

"What was that about?" I asked suspiciously. She bit on her lip as if she wasn't sure she wanted to say.

"Mr. Jones likes to experiment," she finally admitted right as I took a sip of what had to be nectar straight from the gods.

"Experiment how?" I asked with a swallow, suddenly wondering if I was going to regret that.

She sniffed her drink and then sipped it suspiciously, finally swallowing it almost nervously.

We both waited, for what I wasn't sure. I was half expecting her to turn into a frog all of a sudden.

"Mr. Jones fancies himself a bit of a scientist...or maybe a wizard is a better word for what he does," she mused, settling into her seat and taking another long swig of her drink.

Now it was my turn to look at my cup of nirvana suspiciously. "Why did you bring me in here again?" I questioned.

"Oh, it's worth the risk for how good everything tastes, but he did try and give me a love potion once. He swears it's what brought me Rae, but I also got the shits so I'm not so sure about it."

I set my coffee down with wide eyes as she burst into laughter. "I obviously came back though, so I'm not too concerned."

Against my better judgment, I picked up my drink again and resumed enjoying it. I'd probably be better off if I turned into a frog at this point.

It really did taste that good.

Once I'd pushed out of my mind the fact that my drink could have been tampered with by a mad scientist, I asked her about the Town Run.

"Oh, you are in for a treat. It happens every blue moon, and it's just incredible. The wolves—"

"Wait," I said, cutting her off. "It's a wolf run?"

She nodded her head, confused by my reaction. "Didn't you know? Something about the blue moon has the two wolf packs around here going nuts, and they race all together through the streets."

I gaped at her. "And everyone's just okay with that? Is anyone hurt at all?"

Her eyes darkened, something unreadable in their depths. "It's pretty quiet here. There's not a lot of bad things that happen in Amarok. We work hard to keep it that way."

Before I could question her on anything she'd just said,

the door crashed open and a disgruntled looking Rae stormed in.

"Woman! I've been looking all over for you," he barked at a wide-eyed Miyu.

"You know you aren't supposed to sneak off."

Miyu had the grace to look chagrined. For a moment, I thought maybe she'd left him in a compromising sex position or something. She seemed like the type.

But the concern in his gaze as he stared at her, concern... mixed with something that looked like terror. It led me to believe it was something else.

"Everything all right?" I asked, looking between the two of them.

"You need to be careful too. I've heard about your little runs. They're a bad idea right now."

"Because of the wolves?" I asked, confused. Miyu had literally just gotten through telling me how safe the town was. But what I was seeing from Rae didn't support that.

"I guess you wouldn't know since you've only been in town a little while," Rae said, his massive form settling into one of the chairs. He swung an arm behind Miyu, and she curled into him. A pang of envy moved through me, seeing how much they obviously cared about each other. Would I ever stop wishing I had that?

I doubted it.

I could dream though.

At that moment, Rae popped the last bit of Miyu's blueberry muffin into his mouth, and I wasn't envying them at all when Miyu hit him in the stomach and shrilly screamed at him. Evidently, she was passionate about her food. I made a mental note of that.

After Rae had stopped swearing from Miyu hitting him,

they both settled back into each other's embrace as if nothing had happened.

"What were we talking about?" Miyu asked.

I rolled my eyes but couldn't help but grin. "Rae was about to tell me why he was so worried about you sneaking out this morning."

Miyu sobered at that, nodding her head slowly.

"We lost a girl about a month ago. She was just a teenager. She was at a bonfire party, the kids have them constantly during the summer, and then...she was just gone. The whole town searched for her for days. And then we found her..." Rae's voice trailed off, and he turned a little green.

Miyu stroked his back soothingly. "Rae was part of the team that found her," she said quietly. "It...it wasn't pretty. Something had ripped her apart." Rae's body shuddered, and his eyes closed as if he was envisioning it.

"Was it a wolf?" I asked breathlessly, leaning towards them.

Rae shook his head vigorously. "A wolf couldn't do something like that. She'd been torn apart, for fun." He looked out the window towards the tree line where the forest began. "Something's out there. And until we find out what it is..." He turned his attention to Miyu. "You will not leave the house without telling me where you're going. You didn't even bring your phone! If I hadn't seen that we were completely out of coffee, I never would have known where you were."

"I'm sorry, pookie bear," she murmured, tapping him on the nose. "I won't do it again."

I snickered, hardly comprehending that she'd just called the giant Rae pookie bear. The only thing she'd gotten right was the bear part. He was practically as big as a bear.

Rae blushed at the endearment and awkwardly stood up, dragging Miyu with him. "On that note, I need to get ready for my shift. And aren't you doing Mrs. Chankleton's hair in twenty minutes?"

Miyu looked at her watch and screeched in shock. "Fuck, I'm going to be late. And that woman is a beast of timeliness." She began to pull Rae towards the door without another word.

Rae shook his head and waved at me. "See you later today," he told me.

I smiled and waved, watching as they walked out hand in hand. Miyu waved at me frantically as she passed in front of the storefront glass, and I laughed and shook my head at her for what seemed like the millionth time this morning.

As soon as they were gone from sight, my smile faded. What Rae had said was sobering. I looked out towards the woods, taking the last sip of my coffee, remembering how I'd felt like something was watching me from the woods several times.

I really needed to look at whether they had a gym in this town. I didn't really want to spend money on a gym membership, but I didn't really want to die either, so I guess there were tradeoffs. I needed to be better at controlling whatever urge I'd had lately to get out outside and run.

I jumped in surprise when Mr. Jones suddenly appeared beside me. Where the hell had he come from?

"You know I can make you something if you're looking for a man," he told me as he took our empty plates and mugs off the table.

I stood up abruptly and began to slowly back away. "I'm all good on that front," I told him with false cheer. "No man troubles here."

He shook his head as if he knew I was lying. "I'll see you

back here soon, and we'll work something out," he told me, my return a foregone conclusion evidently.

Which, let's be serious, it was. I'd definitely be back. You didn't get an ass like mine by refusing treats, and his coffee and muffins may have been the best I'd ever had.

I waved goodbye and got out of there before I did something crazy like accept a potion from him or something. I didn't trust myself at this point.

As I walked past the coffee shop, I noticed an alley that I hadn't seen before. For a town as small as this one, there was still a lot that I hadn't seen. I could see a green field a block behind the building, so I darted through the alley, nodding to a couple who passed by me. Upon exiting the alleyway, I realized that the green field was actually a cemetery, meticulously kept up with a beautiful view of the mountains and the forest in the distance.

My feet kept me moving as if they had a mind of their own until I saw a weeping couple in front of a recently dug grave. The middle-aged woman was hunched over the dirt, dry racking sobs bursting out of her body, while her husband held her while crying softly himself.

'Delaney Marshall' the gravestone read, listing her death around a month ago.

This must be the teenage girl who was killed.

My heart broke as I watched them, aware I was intruding into a deeply personal moment, but unable to look away.

Something abruptly pulled me forward, single-minded in its purpose, until I was standing right behind the crying couple. The man looked up from his grief in red-rimmed eyes, wondering what I was doing impeding on their misery.

Again, as if someone else controlled me, my hands shot out, and suddenly, they were touching the shoulder of the grieving couple. The woman's sorrow filled the air around us.

Grief poured into me, cold and thick until it was all I could see, touch...taste.

I closed my eyes as it washed over me, and suddenly, a bright white light filled my vision through my closed lids.

And then the feeling of grief...and the light abruptly disappeared.

I was able to take my hand off their shoulders then, and I stumbled backwards, unsure of what had just happened. I was exhausted...drained, like that bright white light had been my essence leaving my body.

The woman turned her head and just stared at me. There was a look of calm serenity on her face where I knew grief had just been.

The man I assumed was her husband looked between the two of us, trying to figure out what just occurred.

"Thank you," the woman whispered in amazement in a choked voice. "I don't know what you just did, but thank you."

I stared at them, confused, finally managing to nod.

And then I ran away, unable to deal with what just occurred. I'd thought escaping Alistair meant I would finally gain control of my life.

But that didn't seem to be the case.

Things were rapidly spiraling out of control, and I was beginning to suspect that I actually was going crazy.

The morning breeze blew through my hair as I twirled a lock around my finger, chewing on my lower lip. Since waking that morning, my mind hadn't stopped going over everything that had happened lately, and trying to make sense of it all only left me more confused.

Yesterday's weird experience with those grieving parents.

The wolves and my attack.

Then there was Daxon, and how I kept dreaming of our kiss.

Not to mention, Wilder and I in the storage room.

I sighed once again that I'd let myself go there with him.

My insane attraction to them both would get me into massive trouble. Apparently, my body refused to behave or listen, and I was addled about my feelings. Arcadia had driven the two men to war, and yet wasn't I just like her with what I'd done with them both? Nothing good could come of this, and in the pit of my stomach, worry churned that I was on the path to destruction.

I shouldn't lead them on, and yet I couldn't stop myself either.

Maybe it was time I left town? Daxon had agreed to pay for my car, and if it was fixed, what stopped me from taking it and leaving everyone and everything behind? I didn't owe them anything...well, aside from the ten grand to Daxon.

The thought of leaving left me shivering as though a storm had ripped through me. Who was I kidding, anyway? Guilt would haunt me for eternity if I took off owing Daxon. Plus, there was the fact that something was happening between the two of us. If I left, I would lose the chance to find out what that was. My thoughts drifted to Wilder, but like always, I pushed them away. I didn't need to find out what was happening between him and I.

As the days passed, I'd begun to feel like I might actually belong in Amarok...and I'd begun to think of Alistair less and less. Which was strange, considering half the town snubbed me. Or had my standards just gotten so low, I was willing to grasp onto any little bit of happiness, no matter how small it was?

Nelly had whispered to me that day, "This place is no good for you, girl. You need to leave."

Now, I couldn't help but wonder if Amarok *was* really good for me. I guessed there was only one way to find out. Stick it out until I could pay off the car by myself...just to be sure I wouldn't be leaving with regrets.

I came up with a plan. I'd continue to get to know Daxon better, stay away from Wilder, and try to think rationally around them both. While I was at it, I wanted to understand what secrets this town held and how it all related to the wolves. And if there really was a monster lurking in the woods, I needed to make sure I stayed alive.

Turning back toward the inn, I made my way inside and

headed upstairs to my room. I'd spotted a laundromat on the main road, and my mountain of dirty clothes was piling up. Tonight, the diner was shut due to the Town Run, and I had every intention of attending the spectacle. It still seemed pretty crazy to me that actual wolves would run through the center of town. It felt like Miyu was trying to pull a prank on me, because that had to be the weirdest thing I'd ever heard.

I laughed to myself as I went around the room and picked up my clothes, stuffing them into a bag before heading out.

The air in the laundromat was damp. It was a large room with nine machines, three against each wall. Plastic black chairs were scattered about in the middle, along with some old magazines. There wasn't a soul in sight, so I strolled across the room and started loading my dirty clothes into a machine before grabbing coins from my pocket for detergent.

Once I had the washer started, I turned to the empty room and grabbed a seat. I had no clue how long I'd been reading through old trashy magazines when the machine finally beeped.

I got up and was switching the clothes to the dryer when someone cleared their throat behind me, making me jump nearly out of my skin.

I hit the start button and twisted around, finding Daxon in the doorway, carrying a coffee and a small brown paper bag.

Despite my earlier resolution to control myself around him, my heartbeat escalated rapidly and even my knees shook at the sight of the gorgeous man. He was dressed in gray pants, stained at the knees as if he'd been kneeling in the dirt. More mud marred his blue tee.

His presence alone had my cheeks feeling hot, and even if my life depended on it, I doubted I could stop myself from smiling. I was embarrassingly aroused, and something had to be wrong with me for me to feel this type of rising need spread through me so quickly.

His gaze tracked me as I crossed the room toward the scattered, plastic chairs.

"Did you come here to wash those clothes of yours? I hope you brought something to change into..." I teased, eyeing his dirty clothes.

"I don't have anything with me, and the owners might object to me hanging around here in the nude," he said with a wink. He stepped inside, his golden hair windblown and messy around his beautiful face, those golden eyes alive with energy. The way he prowled forward left me swallowing the lump in my throat. Every single thing about him screamed sex. "But you probably wouldn't mind, would you, Rune?" he purred, and I swear I about came right there.

Telling myself to calm down was not working, as my breathing sped up the closer he got.

"It's such a shame my wash load is finished," I choked out, trying to come across as cool and confident...and failing miserably.

He shrugged nonchalantly while holding my stare, the intensity behind his eyes never withering. "Your loss. I was ready to strip."

All logic evaporated from my mind, replaced with a naked image of Daxon, all that muscle and golden skin. Judging by the way he'd felt against me the other night, there would be nothing small about him. Fire crawled up between my thighs, and it took every ounce of strength in me to not clench my legs together and make it obvious that such a small comment burned me up in mere seconds. The man was ridiculously hot.

My whole face blushed deeper.

"You're picturing me stripping, aren't you?" He chuckled and flopped down next to me.

I met his gaze and scoffed. "Oh, please. I'm more curious about why you look like you just got done with a mud-wrestling tournament."

He burst out laughing at my comment and shook his head at my ridiculousness. To be fair though, it had been the first thing to pop into my mind.

I never would have been comfortable teasing Alistair, I thought just then. The thought was fleeting, but memorable.

"I'm sorry to say that a strip show is off the table at the moment, but how about a snack? I saw you come in here earlier, so I brought you energy food and a coffee," Daxon asked, bringing me back to the present.

He handed me the brown paper bag as he set the coffee down beside his chair. I caught his eyes on me, waiting for my reaction, though in truth, my thoughts were now a little stuck on the whole idea of Daxon stripping for me.

I opened the bag and immediately was hit by the most delicious scent. My stupid heart began fluttering again at the sweet gesture. "You got me a slice of the vanilla cake I was lusting after yesterday."

I was practically drooling as I stared at it. Seriously though, so much for my health goals. I was going to turn into a walrus in this town because of all the food constantly tempting me.

"I was hoping we could share, but I'm not opposed to watching you eat it yourself as well. You look like you're about to make love to that cake," Daxon joked.

The bag trembled in my hands at his thoughtfulness. "This was really nice of you," I said softly as I tried to blink away the tears that sprung up. They came fast, reminding me I was far from healed from my past.

"It's not a big deal, Rune."

I nodded, ushering the tears at bay, still staring into the bag at the frosting covered treat.

"Hey." Daxon reached over, slipping a bent finger under my chin and lifting my head to face him. Just my luck that a loose tear escaped and rolled down my cheek in that precise moment. "If I knew cake would make you cry, I would have brought you a carrot or maybe some peanuts." He smirked lopsided, coaxing a small laugh out of me.

"It's not the cake." I blinked a few times while he stared into my eyes, his expression so sincere, I struggled to believe it wasn't genuine. When would it stop, this inability to trust anyone? I tried hard to stop doubts from creeping into my mind. But I didn't always win that battle. "Why are you being so kind to me?" I asked.

"Because you deserve so much more. If I ever meet whoever made you think otherwise, I'll pull out his spine to teach him a lesson." His gravelly undertone should have scared me, but it did the opposite. It drew me closer to him. Aside from Nelly, no one ever stood up for me, and to have Daxon do that touched me in a way I never expected.

I sniffled, and he wiped the tear away with his thumb.

"I have no plans to ever cross paths with him again. Now, I just need to find a way to get him out of my head," I said.

"If you ever feel you're in danger, Rune, you come to me. Okay?"

I looked him in the eyes. What was he talking about?

"Rune! I want to hear you agree."

"I heard you, but—"

"There's no negotiation. I won't let anyone harm you."

Who in the world was this man, and why did he actually sound like he cared? "Okay," I finally said. My response came out softly, but it was enough for him to pull his hand away from under my chin and push loose strands out of my face.

"You don't always have to be alone," he murmured.

"I don't know how not to be."

Silence fell between us, and I appreciated that he gave me space.

I reached into the bag and pulled out the cake and then took a bite out of it. Thick icing squished out from both sides, and it was all I could do not to moan at its perfection. My taste buds went haywire from the velvety creamy taste, and my eyes widened as I quickly took another bite.

"It's good, right? Mr. Jones' desserts are addictive."

I handed over the slice to Daxon before I was tempted to eat it all. He took a monstrous bite, and his eyes rolled back, the moan I'd held in sliding on his throat like he might be in ecstasy. I stared at the stunning man, watching as he licked the icing off his lips and fingers. I was finding myself strangely jealous of them.

Something overcame me, and I leaned over, stealing a small bite of the cake right from his hand. "This is incredible."

He came closer, and his mouth touched mine, his tongue licking the icing from my lips. He tasted so sweet that I looped a hand behind his neck and pushed myself closer. Our mouths merged, tongues tangling, sticky icing everywhere.

His entire body hardened against me, his breaths quickening. His passion was a lightning bolt that speared right through my body. Was it normal to feel like this with someone who wasn't your true mate? What would something like this have felt like with Alistair?

His tongue swept through my mouth, tasting all of me, claiming me. I realized then that the more time I spent with Daxon, the more I lost myself.

And that was terrifying, because I'd already lost more pieces of myself than I could count. And I hadn't yet begun to find them.

Closing my eyes, I breathed out. He cupped my face, his fingers in my hair. "I think you should stay in town and not leave."

I flipped open my eyes. My body was on fire with lust, and his words took a minute to absorb into my mind. It was like he could see the earlier thoughts I had this morning. "You do?"

"Do you even realize the impact you have on me? The things I want to do to you. I can't get you out of my mind. I just want a chance for us to explore this...whatever it is."

My breath sped up. His words touched something inside of me. Forget the cake, all I craved now was his hot mouth on my skin, dragging his tongue over every inch of me. I was breathing so heavily, the buttons on my top strained with every inhale like I was in some kind of bodice ripping romance novel. My insides were a mess, a tidal wave of desires building and building.

Finally finding my voice, I said, "I'm not planning on going anywhere until I can pay for the car, or repay you for the car if I need that loan you offered."

Everything about him, from his wicked expression to his sinful mouth, undid me. He ran his tongue across his lips, and I just knew he was well aware of his effect on me...the smug bastard. Against my best intentions, my body trembled with ecstasy as I watched him. He wanted me too, that was very obvious, and if we didn't calm down, I'd end up pinned to the wall, my legs wrapped around him.

I could think of worse things...

"Did I mention the repayment comes with an extremely high interest rate?" he teased me, helping to alleviate the thick fog of lust around us.

"You're too funny." I slid out of his arms and back into my seat, noticing that the rest of the cake sat on the bag in his lap, somehow surviving our ravenous kiss.

"Come back here," he whispered roughly, his hand reaching to pull me back to him. The way he looked at me came with a promise of a question...a question he never asked.

"Are you going to finish the slice?" I said, resisting the urge to throw myself at him. He got the hint that I needed a bit of space, and he handed the rest of the cake to me.

"It's all yours, sweetheart."

I made quick work of finishing the dessert as he climbed to his feet. "I better head back to work," he said. "Will I be seeing you at the Town Run tonight?" He tilted his head to the side, studying the way I licked my lips. Part of me expected him to grab me and continue what he'd started, but he didn't...much to my foolish disappointment.

"I wouldn't miss it, but I'm curious, where do you work?" I heard he owned half the town, so would he really need to work if that were the case?

"Helping out a couple of friends clear out land for a new home they're building across the river," he answered nonchalantly. "But think about what I said earlier. I'm serious about you staying. I could help you find a more permanent place to live here."

His persistence surprised me. He leaned in and kissed

my lips quickly, a guttural sound rolling over his throat. Something primal and animalistic.

His mouth was on fire, and a strange noise spilled from my mouth, something soft and almost submissive. Where had that come from?

With another gorgeous smirk, he strolled out, leaving me behind. I felt a little shell-shocked about what had just happened.

Was this thing between us real, or was I just playing with fire by allowing myself to keep falling deeper for him?

Why would a man like him be interested in me? I'd learned in life that when things were too good to be true... that meant they were. And although it felt incredible to be with him and I was beginning to constantly crave his touch and kiss...I couldn't help but think I was setting myself up for yet another fall to even consider anything between us was possible.

Good things didn't happen to me. I'd learned this time and time again.

It was crazy and idiotic to think otherwise.

I slouched in my chair, licking away a stray bit of icing on my hand, thinking for the hundredth time since I'd come here that I was completely over my head when it came to the men in this town.

~

"*R*une!" Eve waved hysterically at me from the sidewalk. There were people everywhere for the Town Run. It surprised me that she looked so eager to see me outside of work, but I almost too eagerly waved back and made my way over to her.

Large spotlights lit the road, stealing the night away. I

had no idea what to expect tonight, but part of me suspected the run didn't involve actual wolves, as that would be beyond odd...and most definitely dangerous with everyone lining the streets like this.

I wove my way toward Eve, head low and focused on not bumping into anyone while they all refused to move out of my way.

"So glad you're here," she gushed, her cheeks red like she'd been running. She kept glancing around us, almost nervously.

"With everything I've been told about tonight, there was no way I was going to miss out on seeing it myself."

She was nodding very fast, and it was clear her mind was on anything but our conversation.

"Everything all right?" I asked her, both of us moving out of the way of a couple who marched up the street. With limited standing space, trying to avoid bumping into anyone was impossible.

"Oh crap," she whispered under her breath, staring at something down the sidewalk.

Had the run started? I pushed myself up on tippy toes to see over all the heads.

Eve snatched my wrist, dragging me close to her. "You need to do me a favor," she whispered, frantically glancing over her shoulder, then back at me.

"Of course, what's—"

"Just say you're here with me and that you were at my place last night. We were watching movies. Got it?"

I stiffened. "Wait, I—"

Eve straightened instantly and turned her back to me. "Oh, hello, Ms. Fulton. Should be a good night," she said, her voice cracking with nervousness. I glanced past her to find she spoke to the old woman I'd bumped into at the doctor's office. The busybody who wasn't impressed with my presence.

She raised her head, completely ignoring Eve, and glared at me, almost scrunching up her nose at my choice of clothes. Ripped denim shorts and a black tank top. It was hot, and everyone else was dressed basically the same. What was this lady's problem?

With a *humph*, she glanced across to Eve. "I heard you snuck into my house last night while I was out." Her face reddened from anger, her shoulders pulling forward, her floral dress feathering around her throat. "I have told—"

"Your sources must be wrong," Eve interrupted, sounding confident. "I was with Rune last night. We were just chatting about having another movie night after the run. I have no reason to ever go into your home." She feigned shock, which only gained herself a snorting laugh from the woman. Eve glanced over at me with a desperate plea in her eyes.

"Isn't that right, Rune?" she prodded me.

Why was Eve sneaking into the woman's house? To steal something? But being put on the spot and seeing the fury behind Greta's eyes, I had no intention of throwing my friend under the bus. I just hoped this wasn't going to come back and bite me in the ass later.

"Yep, she's right. I love girls' nights. I'm personally into romantic comedies." I felt awkward lying, but I didn't feel too bad remembering how mean the woman had been to me at the doctor's office.

If someone's stare could kill, Greta's would have pinned me to the front window of the bakery behind me and stripped the flesh from my body.

"I may be old, but I'm not stupid enough to believe your lies," she cried out loudly enough to draw attention from the nearby crowd. "Stay away from us, Eve. Your kind isn't welcome." Greta huffed, raised her head, and shoved past both of us, making her way farther up the street.

I turned to Eve. "What the heck was that about? What does your kind mean?"

She snarled, watching Greta march away. "That fucking bitch. I swear she must have been hiding in the bushes, spying on me last night"

"So you did break in? Why?"

Her mouth opened with a response, when a figure stepped out from the shadows and stood extremely close behind her. He gave me an awkward nod, then glanced down to Eve. "Let's go." There was urgency in his voice, and he kept his head low, almost as if trying to appear just like someone else in the crowd.

It was Daniel, the guy who mentioned blood back at the inn and who had been at the doctor's office with Greta. The nurse had told me the old woman had taken him into her home. And here he was with Eve after she'd just gotten the third degree from his foster mother.

It didn't take a rocket scientist to figure out what was going on. Except these two were barely younger than me, and Greta had treated them as if they were fourteen-year-olds. What was I missing?

Why was everything in this town so weird?

"Are you ready to go?" Daniel asked, his gaze taking in the whole street, most likely keeping an eye out for Greta.

Eve smiled cheerfully at me. "If she asks you, tell her I'm in the bathroom or something, okay? Please don't mention, Daniel. I'll explain everything to you later."

Before I could respond, they both turned and hurried down a small alley between two stores, like lovesick teenagers sneaking around. Eve was one of the nicest and most cheerful people I'd ever met. What could she have done to make Greta hate her so much?

I took a step back and was turning to face the street when I bumped right into someone behind me. I flinched to get out of the way. "I'm so sorry."

When I twisted around to see who I had hit, *he* was the last person I expected.

It was Wilder.

He towered over me, hands deep in the pockets of his pants. He wore a V-neck tee under a leather jacket with black jeans, giving him a seriously bad-boy vibe. It definitely matched his personality.

"Oh, it's you," I said, my voice wavering, though I was no longer apologetic for bumping into him. I would have taken Greta over him. Her, I could deal with, but Wilder was a different problem altogether. Greta didn't know what I tasted like...

He reached over and grabbed my arm, then pulled me toward him abruptly.

I instantly shoved against him. "What are you doing? Let me go."

"Calm down," he hissed in my ear, just as someone brushed past my back. I looked around to notice a small group of people were trying to get past me on the sidewalk. With so many people, it made it difficult to stand too far from Wilder.

He released my arm, and I felt a bit silly for reacting that way in all honesty. But it seemed things between Wilder and I were either fire or ice, and I couldn't act normally around him.

I stared up at Wilder, unable to stop myself from comparing him to Daxon. They were so different. They both made me feel more alive...but there was just something about Wilder that was destructive. My feelings for him were...complicated. I was forever scarred by Alistair. What kind of scars would a guy like Wilder leave in me?

I didn't want to find out.

The world I'd known up to now was ruthless and unforgiving, and for a long time, I lived with knowing my future had been stolen from me.

Now for the first time, I felt like I had a chance to take that back. And keeping that control meant I had to be careful with every decision I made, including who I let into my life.

I lifted my head and backed up until my back pressed against a store door. I licked my lips and swallowed, feeling suddenly awkward. My feelings were mirrored in Wilder's unimpressed expression.

"What do you want?" I asked, my voice barely audible.

He remained close...so close, the heat from his body grazed against me. Our close proximity flicked to life flames of desire I was desperate to ignore.

Was it possible to hate and desire someone at the same time?

Unlike the previous times we'd crossed paths, he wasn't snarling at me, which was a nice change of pace at least.

He studied me, and something changed in his gaze. Something familiar grew in his eyes...that same allure he'd possessed back in the storage room in the diner. The hunger, the darkness, the need. He gave me the same dirty expression that had made me forget myself that day.

"What do you want?" I asked again as sweat dripped down my spine from the humid night. The heat seemed to be rising the longer he stared at me, and once again...my heart was banging in my chest.

He smiled faintly then, his eyes flashing a brilliant green.

A guttural sound escaped from his throat as he watched me with a calculating sort of look. And then he leaned forward. "What would you say if I told you I couldn't get it out of my head imagining you bent over my knee as I reddened your ass for constantly pushing me away?"

He said the words coolly, yet fire ignited in his eyes, and I abruptly stopped breathing as images of him spanking me filled my head.

What. The. Hell.

I blushed instantly...because who wouldn't? I was thrown back to how I'd felt in the storage room that day. How I'd had no control. I'd given into my urges, and if he hadn't broken away from me, I knew deep in my gut, I would've let him fuck me against that wall, uncaring of the fact anyone could have come in.

His fingers twirling through the strands of my blonde hair dragged me back from the memory, and he smirked. It was a cruel smile, like he understood the impact he had over me and he loved the torture.

He played with my hair almost as if it were something precious, like he enjoyed the softness against his skin. What was I supposed to be doing right now? My emotions were ruling me, tugging me down every path but the one I was supposed to be on.

He cupped the side of my face, his fingers on my cheek, tipping my head back to look him in the eyes. "Maybe I was wrong. Maybe what the town needs is a little bit of your wild," he whispered.

I blinked at him, my chest squeezing like it was being squashed. "A little bit of my wild? What do you mean?"

He hesitated at first, and I studied the conflict in his gaze as though he battled between telling me what he meant or just being aloof...or an asshole like always.

I leaned against the storefront, unable to believe what he'd just told me. Wild. Me. Like the two could ever go together.

His words were confusing. From the beginning, he'd made it clear that he wanted me gone. And now...it seemed like he was almost asking me to stay.

Nothing was making sense, and exhaustion hit me, wearing me down. I was so tired of all the games. Alistair had played enough games with me to last a lifetime. And I couldn't take any more.

I pushed off the wall, ready to tell him goodbye for good, when up ahead, the people mulling around burst into cheers.

A dark blur zipped up the street at blinding speed.

I jerked my head up. "Did you just see that?"

The locals around us bustled into excited chatter, more of them pushing forward to see the road. I brushed past Wilder, needing to look closer. Then right before my eyes, a gray wolf bolted up the street...a real-life wolf. He ran fast, the wind in his ash colored fur, determination on his face.

I was stunned, my jaw dropping open.

Was this really happening?

A thunderous sound came from down the street. I bent forward to peer past the masses.

More wolves ran up the road, all of various colors, grays, blacks, tawny, their fur smooth and shiny. They all panted, tongues hanging out, racing each other to be first. There had to be close to twenty animals. Their movements were swift and elegant, each step purposeful, their bodies muscular and confident.

A tinge of fear sliced through me to see these wild

animals rushing past me. What stopped one from lunging at the crowd?

The people cheered them on though, obviously not having my concerns. It felt like I'd just stepped into an episode of *The Twilight Zone*.

There were real wolves running through the town. How could this be happening?

I continued to watch in amazement as the wolves rushed past. When they got around the corner, they looped back and ran the opposite direction until wolves were running both ways. I'd never heard of anything like it. It was as if someone was controlling their movements, synchronizing them into a beautiful dance that I knew I wouldn't forget for as long as I lived.

Why wasn't this in the news? Why weren't there a million people crowding these streets trying to see what must be one of the world's wonders?

"It's beautiful, isn't it?" Wilder suddenly said next to me, reverently. I'd forgotten he was still here for a moment.

"The most beautiful thing I've ever seen," I admitted, unable to look away from the sight. "How long do they do this? And why?"

Out of the corner of my eye, I saw Wilder smile and stifle a laugh as if he was in on a joke I wasn't. He pointed up to the sky where the blue moon was illuminating the night above the mountains.

"There's something about the moon. It drives the wolves to run. It's been this way for as long as I can remember."

His words made me think of my own urge to run since coming to this town. It always sat there, right beneath the skin, an ever-present urge that I tried my best to control, as I hadn't found a gym yet and I'd had enough warnings to be careful when running outside.

"You've lived here all your life, right?" I asked as we both stood there watching.

He hummed and then nodded. "Born and raised. I suppose I'll die here as well."

There was a bit of melancholy in his words, as if that was a big disappointment to him. Which was surprising since he allegedly owned half the town. Wilder didn't seem the type to be forced to do anything, so why did he seem upset about staying here?

"It seems like there's more to that statement," I said carefully, sure that at any minute, this fragile peace we were in while watching the wolves run would be shattered and it would be back to business as usual.

There was a long silence, and I watched in amazement as a ginormous, freaking gorgeous snow-white colored wolf with one blonde paw weaved his way in and out of the animals, taking his place in the front. The other wolves fell in line easily behind him, recognizing their apparent leader. Wilder frowned at the sight.

"I'm sure you've noticed that new people don't really come to this place. But when they do, they don't leave. Everyone you see around you has been here since birth. We all carry the weight of our family traditions on our back, and any other path is discouraged."

Wilder was silent again, but his silence was filled with a million unspoken things. He sighed and pushed his hair out of his face. I stared distractedly at the way the moon settled across his features, turning him into some sort of dark prince that I noticed others had a difficult time tearing their gazes from as well. If there was anyone who could distract away from the gorgeous predators continuing to dart past us, it was him.

"I went away for college actually," he finally said. He didn't look that much older than me, so I wondered how long he'd been back. "I got a scholarship for basketball." He looked away from the wolves, his emerald eyes serious as if it was important to him for me to know this about him. "I was good. So good, there was all this talk about me going pro. I suddenly had this whole other life set out for me."

Something in his cheek pulsed at the thought.

"And then I was back here on break, and Arcadia had called me, sobbing about how she missed me or something, and that she was in trouble and needed me to come pick her up."

He laughed bitterly at the memory.

"She wasn't in trouble. She was drunk, at some bar two towns over, picking a fight with some local drug dealers who wanted blow jobs in exchange for their blow. Of course, being the idiot I was, who never could say no to that girl, I stood up for her alleged honor. I beat the crap out of the three of them and walked her out of there to my car. Before we got too far out of town, they came after us and side-swiped my car."

I gasped, thoroughly entranced at his story, while imagining my own recent crash.

"My leg got struck with the impact, my tibia shattered to pieces."

"And you couldn't play after that?" I asked, an ache in

my heart as I watched him, knowing he was still mourning that moment.

He shook his head. "I've always been a fast healer," he said in a gravelly voice. "I would have been as good as new the next season. But the drug dealers were actually the sons of the local leaders of that town, the mayor and the police chief of all things. The police of that town were the first to find us, and they read me my rights as I was wheeled into surgery for the injuries to their boys. They made a huge deal about it. They didn't care what I had to say or what had actually happened, or that their boys had run us off the road." His body shook angrily at the memory. "The university didn't want to have anything to do with me after that, and no one else would take a chance on me, not with charges still pending for the next year. And so I came back here, took classes at the local college. And that's that."

He laughed again as we watched a wolf nip at the leg of another wolf as they raced by. "My life was ruined, and the girl I was trying to help, the girl I'd been in love with for so long that I couldn't even remember when it started...she lost another man's baby. Just the cream on top of everything."

My stomach churned. So that was what happened. Arcadia hadn't gotten rid of Daxon's baby, she'd lost it in the crash...which she was in with another man. Fierce hatred rushed through me at the thought of everything she'd done. But these guys had also been idiots. Was her pussy made of gold or something? I felt sick just thinking about how much they'd loved her.

I realized that Wilder had said my name, and I looked at him, unable to meet his eyes for some reason. "I know all about losing your future," I finally said to him, my body trembling as I remembered when I'd lost mine.

I didn't remember anything after Alistair severed our mate bond. When I woke up and found myself in a closet-sized room, I had no idea of how I'd gotten there. The only thing I knew was that I didn't walk into the room myself because I hadn't been able to move last night.

It felt...like I was dying. There was no other way to describe it. Like someone had taken my soul and ripped it in half. Did Alistair have the other half? Is this what he was feeling too? Or did the rejector somehow escape the pain of the rejected? Wouldn't that be a cruel twist of fate.

Have you ever tried to survive with your soul split apart, stuck in the agony of a lost relationship only multiplied by ten million because the person you'd lost was the only one in the world for you?

And where was my mother? I felt like a child again, desperate for the warmth of her arms and the reassurance that everything would be all right, even if every word she said was a lie.

I wanted to die. I'd never met a rejected wolf before, and now I knew why. Because it was not survivable. If I'd seen one on the street, I would have seen a ghost, so alone and lost that you would look right past them, not realizing you had in fact passed a real person.

Maybe I had already died. The girl I was yesterday was certainly nowhere to be found. There was no hope for her to rise from the ashes. That girl had been burned until everything was gone, and a new life was impossible.

At least that's what it felt like right now.

What would become of me?

I faintly remembered being told I would be serving in Alistair's house, but thinking back on that now, that didn't seem right.

Alistair at least had to have cared for me enough to not force me to be around him now. Right? Hadn't I seen that recognition in his eyes when he looked at me, the one that said I was the only *one for him? Why would he want to be reminded of what he'd lost?*

A part of me was still foolishly holding out for the fact that all of this was just a bad nightmare, a product of the nerves I'd experienced prior to arriving at the dinner. I was waiting for the door to be opened and Alistair to be there, holding out his arms, letting me know that everything was fine, that our fairy tale was about to begin.

Growing up, I'd had nightmares constantly, images I didn't understand had taken over my nights. Waking up every morning was a relief.

I prayed that somehow, this was the same.

I was a fool.

The door opened, and a stiff-looking woman who looked like she smelled something rotten stood there. She was dressed in an old-fashioned black maid's uniform with lace on her freshly pressed white apron. "Come with me," she ordered, her tone cold and unyielding.

I got up and obediently followed her from the room, not sure what else to do. I was in the alpha's mansion...I thought. Everything around me was so decadent, I didn't know what else it could be.

"Have you seen my mother?" I asked when the silence became too much.

She muttered something under her breath. "As you know, your mother left last night after your shame was announced. I don't blame her in the least."

"As I know?" I asked, a cry caught in my throat. She wouldn't have left me, not when I needed her so badly. There had to have been a mistake.

She gave me an impatient look. "You were explained all of this last night. Playing stupid will get you nowhere here. You need to accept that this is your new life and try to make the best of it."

I had so many more questions as it became clear nothing of last night had in fact been a dream, but I got the feeling she wouldn't be answering any.

We reached what looked like a main living area. All I could see out the window was an inky blackness, meaning that somehow, I'd been asleep an entire day. A solemn looking man dressed in a pristine black suit stood up when we entered.

"Is this her?" he asked the woman, not looking at me once.

"Yes. He wants it done right away," she answered.

Who wanted what done right away? What were they talking about?

Another man entered the room dressed in the all-black uniform of the alpha's enforcers. Panic hit me then, and I struggled against the women's suddenly iron-clad grip. I managed to break away, but then two enforcers were on me and I couldn't move at all. I watched as the man in the suit walked over to the fireplace and picked up a metal rod that had been leaning against the stone. He picked it up and the dread only grew when I saw that there was some kind of brand at the end of the rod. He put the rod into the roaring fireplace, not taking it out until the brand, which looked a little like a snake wrapped around a wolf, was a burning red color. He began to chant something in Latin, and the brand began to glow even brighter. I began to struggle as ferociously as I could against the enforcers' grip, my cries filling the air. I couldn't let that brand touch me, I couldn't.

"Please," I begged, but my cries fell on deaf ears.

The man stopped chanting and walked over to me, finally looking at me with a blank, pitiless gaze.

These people were all monsters.

"Mother. Alistair. Alpha," I cried out, sure that this was all a mistake. Someone was going to come to save me, they had to.

When the man holding the brand was standing in front of me, Alistair appeared from down a hallway, across the room.

"Please, help me!" I cried out to him. He just stared at me though, emotionless, like I was nothing to him...like I'd never been anything to him.

"Rune Celeste Esmaray, you have been found unworthy for the gift the moon goddess has bestowed upon your blemished soul. With this mark, your wolf will be severed from you, protected from the shame you would bring upon it."

Before the meaning of the words could fully sink in, my blue dress that I was still wearing from the night before was ripped open, and the brand was thrust against the skin on my back. I screamed at the unspeakable pain, my body frozen as agony coursed through my veins. After what felt like hours, the brand was removed and I was dropped to the floor, my whole body shaking with adrenaline for what I'd just experienced.

I begged the moon goddess for death. But it never came.

And my wolf was locked inside of me from that day on, never to be freed.

The brand against my back was gone by the time I looked in a mirror, but I could still feel its curse under my skin.

"Rune." Wilder's voice cut through my remembered pain, and I stared at him blankly, trying to remember what we'd been talking about.

A howl ripped through the air, and everything came back.

"Rune, baby. Are you all right?"

I belatedly realized I was in Wilder's arms, and there were tears streaming down my face.

I breathed in his unique scent for a second, trying to ground myself as embarrassment seeped in at what had just occurred.

I finally pulled away from him, struggling to look at him

and wanting to go hide in my room. Any wonder I'd felt at the wolves running past had disappeared.

Wilder tipped up my chin so I was forced to look at him, and I was surprised to see rage etched across his features. His eyes...

They weren't normal looking. They were glowing. I stepped back in shock, suddenly feeling something sharp scratch and tear at my skin where Wilder had been holding me around the waist still. He let me go suddenly, and I gasped when I saw sharp claws extending out from his fingers.

"Rune, run," he growled desperately, and all I could do was stand there for a second as his teeth began to lengthen in his mouth and his nose began to extend forward.

Wilder was a fucking shifter. I'd escaped from one hell only to find myself in another.

With a scream, I darted away, blindly pushing past the crowds of people that were still watching the wolves.

Were those even wolves? I doubted that now. This whole town was probably filled with shifters.

I was such a fool.

My breath came out in gasps as I ran to the edge of town, expecting any moment for someone to grab me. I didn't know where to go...what to do.

So of course, I found myself in the motherfucking woods, right where I'd been warned time and time again not to go.

I doubted whatever was in these woods was as dangerous to me as what I'd left behind in town though. I could feel rivulets of blood sliding from the scratch Wilder had made in my skin.

Howls suddenly filled the night, and I stopped in place, not knowing which direction to go. Were they everywhere? I clamped a hand over my mouth, trying to stifle my breathing and the screams that were threatening to emerge.

"Rune, baby," I heard Daxon call from somewhere nearby just then.

I darted behind a tree and crouched at its base, hoping somehow, I wouldn't be seen.

He was one of them. I knew he was. Wilder and he were both the alphas of their packs. I was such an idiot. So many things made sense now, all the little jokes everyone had made.

I'm sure they'd all gotten quite a laugh at my idiocy.

Wolves could see in the dark. Daxon was probably watching me nearby. Shivers slid across my skin, and tears fell down my face. I'd vowed never to find myself near a shifter again. And here I was.

"Boo," Daxon suddenly whispered across the skin on the back of my neck, and this time, a scream filled the air around me.

He didn't touch me, he just stood there, staring at me, an unfamiliar predatory look in his gaze like he was just daring me to run.

I held up my hands in front of me. "Please, I won't tell anyone. Just let me go."

"It didn't have to be like this, you know. We were going to ease you into this, convince you to stay before we told you our secrets," Daxon told me.

"I'm one of you. You have nothing to fear from me."

"We still don't even know how you made it here without someone stopping you. We have guards in place to make sure no one passes into the town borders without our permission."

"It was just my luck," I whispered, feeling suddenly like I had no idea who the man standing in front of me was.

"We can't let you go. I'm sure you can understand," he said, taking a step towards me.

"What? Daxon, please. I—"

Something sharp pricked my neck just then, inserted by someone who'd crept up behind me while I was distracted with Daxon.

My last image was of Daxon staring down at me, his golden eyes glowing...

Everything went black after that.

I awakened to darkness with a jarring gasp in my throat, and I jolted upright in bed. For a moment, I thought I was back in Alistair's house, in my tiny bed in my dark room. I curled up, trembling. Alistair would be here any second...I'd be punished for sleeping in. My heartbeat pounded in my ears, and every terrifying second that passed had me curling up tighter, dread swallowing me.

Just then, the sweet laughter from Carrie came from somewhere downstairs, followed by Jim's boisterous chuckle. A calmness settled over me. I was safe, as far from Alistair as possible.

I laid there for a moment, blinking, staring at the dresser across the room from me. I was at the inn. The blinds were pulled shut, drenching everything into darkness.

How did I get back to my room?

What happened came trickling into my memory... slowly. The Town Run, Wilder turning into a fucking wolf, and me fleeing from him...from the whole town. Daxon had found me in the woods. And then everything faded to black.

My heart thumped in my chest at the memories.

I froze in front of Daxon, not able to move a muscle as if he'd cast a spell. I felt sick to my stomach thinking about the way the world came crashing down around me at his words.

We can't let you go, Daxon had said, and the look in his eyes would haunt me forever.

He'd lied.

Everyone in this place had.

I couldn't help but think of the time we'd spent together over the last few weeks. Our date, the way he'd made me laugh, those kisses that were forever burned into my memory. Those moments felt so real that my throat choked up just thinking of them. But after last night, I realized he'd been playing me the whole time. They all had.

My breath caught in my chest as hate coursed through me.

Why hadn't I seen what was right in front of me?

And now it was too late.

They were all shifters...every single one of them. And I had no clue.

What if they'd been in contact with Alistair this whole time and this had just been one elaborate trap?

I was so fucked.

I shoved the blanket off my legs and scrambled out of bed, noticing I still wore my ripped denim shorts and the black tank top from last night. At least my shoes had been removed. I padded right to the door and grabbed the handle. To my surprise, it opened up with ease. I had expected it to be locked. When I stuck my head out, there were only the usual sounds of voices downstairs, nothing out of the ordinary and no one standing guard near my door either.

Quickly, I shut the door and marched across my room to the window.

Sweeping open the curtains, the morning sunlight blinded me at first. I blinked through it and glanced down to the lawn and the nearby river down below. I didn't see any guards waiting to stop me from leaving there either. Daxon had mentioned protectors watching the town though. I'm sure they were out there, waiting out of sight, and they'd be on high alert to keep an eye out for me if I tried anything.

Crossing my arms tightly, I stood there, staring outside, my teeth chattering. I still couldn't believe how everything had fallen apart yesterday, or that I'd somehow walked right into a wolf pack community.

This was just another example of how I was cursed.

I clenched my jaw, my heart hammering as the walls seemed to close in around me. The majestic view in front of me suddenly didn't look so serene. I had traded one prison for another. And a prison, no matter how beautiful, was still a prison.

I kept rubbing my hands on my arms, itching all over. I walked to the bed and grabbed a pillow, hurling it at the window as I screamed with frustration. Anger burned up my insides.

"Fuck!"

The pillow didn't make it to the window, instead, it crashed into my water bottles on the table, sending them sprawling and clattering to the floor.

We were going to ease you into this, convince you to stay before we told you our secrets.

From the moment I arrived, I had sealed my fate, and they had no intention of letting me go.

My whole body trembled, and the edges of my eyes feathered with darkness...with panic crawling over me. There had been a period of time where I'd had panic attacks constantly, and I could tell one was coming on right now.

I rushed into the bathroom and splashed my face with cold water before cupping some in my hands and drinking it. I took deep breaths, trying to calm down.

Gripping the sink, I stared into the mirror at my red rimmed eyes, at my messy hair. "Why?" I whispered to my reflection, wondering how one girl could have so much bad luck.

Running from one monster and into the arms of another wasn't exactly the most brilliant move. Yet that was exactly what I'd done.

My heart squeezed as I ran through my options. I was pretty sure no amount of pleading was going to get me out of this situation. I checked outside the window again. Still no one out there.

Hadn't I known both of the men would spell trouble for me? And like always, hadn't I ignored my own instincts?

I trembled with fury, wearing a path on the floor as I paced. Anger flared under my skin each time Daxon's words swept over my mind. They churned in my thoughts, deepening the ache of feeling trapped.

A scream lashed my throat as I thought about what I could have done differently last night. I should have taken matters into my own hands and gone to get my car. It had been three weeks, surely it was at least drivable by now, if not all the way fixed. In a car, at least I wouldn't have been hunted. Maybe I would have gotten away.

I kicked myself for being blinded by a fantasy. Who wouldn't have been overwhelmed by two guys who looked like Wilder and Daxon though? For a mess like me, their hot touch and sweet words had been like kryptonite. I cringed thinking of how I'd cried in front of them both. They must have gotten a good laugh from that.

The overwhelming urge to lash out and hurt them was

heavy in my chest. My throat constricted each time I thought about my arrival in town, the clues I'd seen about the residents not being humans, but my brain just hadn't been able to accept that all the clues pointed to them being shifters.

My pulse pounded. I couldn't stay in my room a second longer or I'd go mad. I grabbed my sandals and my bag, and headed out. At the bottom of the stairs, my body tensed. Was I ready to look Jim and Carrie in the eyes? Right now, their kindness felt like a lie, even though something in my heart told me that wasn't the case.

Please let them not be there.

Peering around the corner of the stairs and into the main bar section, I spied Jim vanishing into the kitchen. There was no sign of Carrie. This was my chance. I bolted toward the door and hurried outside into the scorching heat.

I swung my attention left and right across the lawn, but no one came running toward me. I kept picturing being dragged off and locked up in a small room for the rest of my life, any chance of freedom a distant and impossible dream.

I wasn't going to let that happen.

Unlike the time Alistair took everything from me, where I'd been too young and broken by the loss of my mate to do anything, there was no way I was going to sit back and let anyone ever steal my freedom again. I was sure as hell going to find a way to leave this town.

Shivers crept down my skin just then. I looked out across the river and woodlands around me, unable to shake the feeling I was being watched. I had no doubt that the moment I stepped foot in the forest, I'd be stopped.

Unsure where to go, I began to walk, needing to move so I could think clearly. I started heading down the main street, the buildings no longer seeming so quaint in this new world I'd found myself in. I kept looking around, still expecting to be stopped. Was this some kind of game to try and give me a false sense of security and lure me into attempting an escape?

An ache sliced down my back, the tension in my muscles only getting worse as I continued to think about Daxon's words.

I wanted to run.

To cry.

To hide.

But I couldn't.

The streets were empty of people, only a few customers in the stores I passed. Everyone had been drinking pretty heavily the night before for the Town Run I'm sure they were still recovering.

Before I knew it, I swung down the alleyway leading to the small grocery store. Maybe a bag of disgustingly unhealthy snacks to drown in was exactly what I needed, because I was going to go crazy at this rate. A giant tub of ice cream and a bag of Doritos was a must.

Nothing seemed innocent anymore. Had it been a coincidence that a wolf had crossed the road in front of me? Had I been lured here from the beginning?

Purposefully breathing slower to calm myself, I rubbed my arms and looked around as an older woman emerged from the grocery store. She threw me a quick glance, and then hurried away.

Was she a shifter?

That was a stupid question. Of course, she was. Was she watching me, like all the others, to ensure I didn't go anywhere? My nerves danced just thinking about it.

The front glass doors slid open for me, and I stepped

inside the grocery store, greeted by the coolness of an air conditioner and white sterile walls. Five rows of shelves filled with foods and supplies lay beyond the one cash register, where a young girl checked someone out. It was a small place, but I guess it fit this small town.

I collected a shopping cart, then pushed it down the first aisle, looking for what I wanted. The rows of food helped distract me. I was a second away from falling into a fetal position and never getting back up if I didn't calm down.

I needed to bide my time, act like I was resigned to my fate, find their weaknesses, and then make my escape fast. I could do this.

I shoved the cart forward, and started adding Oreos, at least three packets, and a bag of nacho cheese Doritos. On the third aisle, I filled up on a pack of peach flavored iced tea. Always the peach.

As I reached up to grab one more pack, because you can never have enough, someone rammed their cart into mine, sending it smacking into my hip.

"Ouch." I whirled around, still clutching the bottle of ice tea, and rolled my eyes when I saw it was Arcadia. Of course it was her. Just what I needed today…a little dose of psycho.

My stomach dropped at the prospect of having to deal with her. That was when I noticed that while my shopping consisted of junk food, she had half a dozen bags of dog food, which was strange to say the least.

"Watch yourself," she snarled, pulling her cart away from mine, then steering past me, her upper lip curling over pristine white teeth. "Get in my way again, and you won't see me coming. I've already warned you once that no one wants you here." She stormed down the aisle, her heels click clacking against the linoleum, her skin tight red skirt curving over her round ass and tapering down to her knees. Quite the outfit for the grocery store.

I arched a brow, half taken aback, half amused by her threat. Had she not received the memo that I was trapped here? I would gladly take up any offer to get out of here.

Wilder's words flared over my mind about their past, about the lost pregnancy, about the heartache she'd left behind. I stiffened, shaking my head in frustration that there was a part of me that seemed to still care what she'd done to Daxon and Wilder.

Setting the ice tea into my cart, annoyance burst through me. "No need to be a bitch, Arcadia," I called out to her.

"Fuck you!" She swung back toward me, not someone to leave things alone, and she whacked her cart into another one belonging to a younger couple near her. They yelped at the impact, glaring at Arcadia.

She started yelling at them, throwing her hands in the air, "Watch where you're going, idiots. You're not the only ones in this store."

The husband stepped forward, talking to her calmly with words I could barely decipher, while his wife frowned at Arcadia's erratic behavior.

I watched the exchange, amusement replacing annoyance. At least it wasn't just me she had a problem with. The commotion drew the attention of the store manager, an older man, who got into the argument with Arcadia, pointing at her cart. She didn't let up though, only getting louder.

Instantly, something tugged at my chest, and I found myself stumbling toward them, my feet seeming to have a mind of their own. A slither of panic pierced through my chest over my lack of control. What was happening?

The store manager noticed my approach and shook his

head for me to stay back. But it was too late, and I instinctively placed a hand on Arcadia's arm. Thickness filled the air, so heavy and overbearing, it washed over me with tainted rage, my blood boiling, my chest on fire from the fury erupting through my veins.

Everyone looked at me, bewildered by what I was doing. Arcadia jerked her attention toward me, and if looks could kill, I'd be long dead.

Energy pulsed in the air around me, and I shut my eyes to cope with the darkness pouring into me. In seconds, a bright light flashed behind my eyelids and vanished as quickly as it came. The anger tainting the air evaporated.

"What did you do to me?" Arcadia's voice came out soft, and almost sorrowful, a tone I never would have expected to hear from her.

I pulled my hand back as I slid open my eyes, having no clue how this kept happening to me. Just like it had at the cemetery grounds with the mourning couple. Everyone stared at me as if I'd grown a horn, and I took a few steps back, not sure what to do.

Arcadia blinked at me, completely stunned. All the anger in her expression had melted away. Only a serene look filled her eyes, one of calmness and confusion.

"What just happened?" the store manager asked.

Arcadia stared at me blankly.

I shook my head, my lungs constricting, breath struggling. I was terrified at what had just occurred. I'd written off the cemetery incident, sure that it was just coincidence.

But I couldn't ignore this.

It made no sense, nothing did, and the longer the four of them stared at me, the more panic I felt.

"I-I don't know." Lowering my head, I ran out of the

store, leaving my cart and its contents behind. I sprinted toward the inn, shaking the entire way.

Something must be broken inside me, because normal people...normal shifters didn't behave like that. I didn't stop running until someone stepped in my way on the sidewalk, blocking my path.

I stumbled to a stop, breathing heavily, and looked up.

Wilder stood in front of me. Inky hair framed his face, strands hanging over one eye. Dense stubble coated his jawline, and those deep green eyes darkened as his thick eyebrows narrowed. Perfect, full lips made for kissing drew my attention, and I quickly looked away. I noticed he looked exhausted. Like he'd been awake all night.

Fuuuuuck. "W-what do you want?"

"In the mood to listen this morning?" The intensity behind his gaze pierced into me.

He stood broad, arms stiff by his sides, telling me had no intention of leaving until we spoke.

"That depends. Are you going to allow me to leave afterwards?" I asked snottily.

His silence spoke volumes.

"Then I'm not in the mood," I answered with a sigh.

"Let's go and talk somewhere private, Rune."

I stiffened, glaring at him. "I said no."

"And I'm not leaving until we do."

I gave him my best death glare, raised my chin, and turned away, having had enough. Before I took one step, he grabbed my arm at the elbow and wrenched me back to him. I spun back around, stopping short of colliding into his chest.

Driving my gaze up to meet his, I hissed, "You can't go around manhandling me."

"I can when you aren't being reasonable."

His response made me furious, and I pushed against him, which was a little bit like trying to move a mountain.

"I just want to talk," he said, frustrated. Wilder released me and opened his palm up, offering it to me like a peace treaty.

He was tall and formidable standing there. The black tee he wore revealed every angle and curve of his muscles, and my stupid heart couldn't stop from thinking how attractive he was.

"What do you say, Rune? Just let me explain some things."

Tension dug deep in my shoulder blades, and I couldn't bring myself to respond at first. I just listened to the beating of my heart in my ears as I tried to think.

I sighed finally, feeling like I didn't really have a choice. And this could work towards my plan, letting them think I was going to cooperate. I would hear Wilder out, knowing full well he would force it on me regardless. And maybe he would tell me something that would help me to get out of here.

"Fine, let's make this short," I said.

He grabbed my hand in his, his expression blank, and he rushed me across the street, my feet practically flying from how fast he moved. We darted down an alleyway and emerged in a field with a dirt road and a few houses dotting the land. Most of them were small and made of brick, and a few even had white picket fences.

Wilder drew me toward the only home that was two-story. Deep brown walls, black frames around the windows. The front yard had a short lawn, and a stone path leading from the street to the front door. There weren't any flowers or decorative pieces, or a fence. He paused at the black arched door and unlocked it with keys from his pocket.

When he pushed it open, he stepped inside and waved for me to join him. The hallway lit up from the sunlight behind me, revealing a grand staircase heading upstairs. It was modern, simplistic, white walls, fancy moldings, and a metal chandelier. Exactly what I'd expect from a bachelor pad.

He shut the door behind me and swung into a living room. It was the bare essentials in there, no images or paintings on the wall, not even a television. Just a coffee table, black leather couch, and a bookshelf covering one wall.

I walked over to the window, staring out at the quiet street, the sunlight making it appear like another gorgeous day where everything was perfect.

"Talk," I said, folding my arms over my chest, glad he decided to sit on the corner of the couch, legs parted, his hands on his thighs, and far enough from me.

"How much do you know about wolf shifters?" he asked me in a soft tone.

I shrugged. "Same as every other shifter I'm sure. Lycans live in the shadows of humans, mainly controlled by the moon. Some can't shift outside those three days a month."

"But there's many who've managed to gain control of their wolves without the moon," he added.

I nodded, having seen Alistair and others in his pack often going for hunts outside full moons to ensure they held control of their wolves.

"Why are you giving me a history lesson?" I asked, not sure where he was going with this.

"Rune, babe, are you aware that there are four wolf shifter breeds in the world?"

I blinked at him, unsure I heard right. "What do you mean by four? I'd been taught that Lycans were the only ones, the superior race." My breath caught in my lungs, and my voice came out slightly scratchy from the shock of his implication.

Wilder got to his feet and came over to where I stood and took my hand. He led me to the couch. "Sit."

He flopped down and eyed me to do the same, which I reluctantly obeyed.

"What did you mean by four wolf breeds?" I pressed.

"Four types exist in our world. You're familiar with the Lycan because you came from a Lycan pack."

My heart sank at what I was hearing. Four wolf breeds. No freaking way. Was there anywhere I could go that would be safe if there were that many out there?

My parents, Alistair, everyone I'd grown up with...they never talked about anything but the Lycan. How could no one have told me there were other kinds? I'd lived in a bubble, in a vacuum, completely blind to the world. I felt my chest tighten, and I hugged my middle.

"I'm a Lycan too," Wilder said, interrupting my thoughts gently, drawing my attention back to him as he leaned closer, elbows pressed against his thighs. "We're the most powerful of all the breeds. We're pretty unstoppable when we battle." There was a cocky look in his gaze, and I rolled my eyes.

"What about Daxon?" I asked with a frown. I just knew he wasn't a Lycan, not with the way Wilder was explaining this. He just seemed...different.

"He's a Bitten. They aren't controlled by the moon, and they have full power over their wolves. They're extremely powerful healers when they're injured. There's not much known about their breed historically though. I once heard that the Bittens might be the first original wolf shifter breed, but who knows." Wilder shrugged his shoulders as if he couldn't care less.

I was frozen in place, my mouth hanging open. The world seemed even more intimidating with all of this news. Alistair treated me as his puppet, locked away from the world, and I cursed him for still making my life shit even when he wasn't around.

"The third kind is a Totemic wolf. They're created when a human is bitten by their kind, or transformed by magic. And last are the Fenrir wolves, the most aggressive of the four kinds and definitely the breed you want to keep your distance from at any cost."

When he looked at my confused face, his expression was sympathetic. I couldn't pull my gaze from his. "Your pack and Daxon's live in this town, don't they?"

He nodded. "He resides across the river, and my Lycans are on this side. We've worked out a way to live in harmony. The territory on their side of the river belongs to them, and this side past the town is my jurisdiction. The town is a safe zone for everyone." He paused, studying me. "I know this is a lot to take in, and when we have more time, I want to understand more about how you don't know any of this."

I stayed quiet for a long moment, studying his face, trying to take in everything I'd discovered. Of course it made sense that there would be more breeds in hindsight, but my jaw clenched with how much I'd been lied to all my life.

Wilder watched me. "Are you okay?"

I stood up. "It's just a lot to take in. Maybe I should go."

His gaze never left me, and I shivered thinking of how out of touch I felt in the world. I didn't belong anywhere. Not with my pack, as Alistair made sure of, not with the humans, and definitely not here.

Alistair had once labeled me an outcast, and I felt that more now than I ever had.

"Okay, four kinds of wolves aside, why can't I leave here?

I obviously grew up knowing our kind has to be kept secret," I told him bluntly, part of me expecting him to respond with a cryptic message, giving me nothing.

He stood alongside me, and I tried not to think of how small I was compared to him. "To keep you protected."

I snorted. "Right. You're keeping me prisoner to keep me safe. That makes perfect sense." I laughed bitterly. "Thank you, but I think I'm good."

"You need us."

His expression gave absolutely nothing away, but his words were a warning, a threat to me.

"What I need is to leave," I said.

He slid a finger under my chin, and my skin heated up everywhere he touched me. His thumb stroked over my lips, pulling at the flesh, and he stared down at me with hunger building in his gaze that seemed out of place for the situation.

My body reacted so quickly, it surprised me at the intensity of the thumping desire that came from his touch.

"We aren't finished," he told me. "There's so much more I want you to understand. Your wild is beautiful, Rune, but your stubbornness is only going to get you into trouble. You're not going anywhere."

His voice was calm but firm, and I couldn't work out if he was referring to me not leaving the town...or his house. An elated feeling spread through my veins with his touch. I couldn't explain how part of me wanted to strangle him, but another part couldn't stop looking at his lips, craving them.

"Why do you care what happens to me?" I asked, genuinely curious. Since arriving in town, we'd been two forces constantly at war. Everything between us had been... difficult, but the man standing before me right now was different.

Was this all part of the game?

"Do you want me to spell it out?" He ran his thumb over my lips again, but he never gave me the chance to respond. Because his mouth pressed against mine.

I shuddered in his arms, my body softening against him, and all my determination to keep him at arm's length now floated away.

He kissed me with the intensity of an inferno. He was fire and I was his flame, igniting, roaring to life. I pressed closer, grasping onto his tee, kissing him back, pushing myself up on my toes to reach him easier. The world faded around us. Nothing else mattered when my body buzzed with this overwhelming energy. I was lost, consumed, feelings I didn't understand shooting through me.

How could I feel so much so quickly for someone like Wilder?

When he broke from our kiss and I drew in sharp, shallow breaths, I couldn't remember anything but us.

"Yes. Say it," I ordered, answering his earlier question. "What exactly do you want from me?"

His arms scooped under my knees and back, and he had me off my feet, his lips on mine again.

"I want it all, Rune. Everything you'll give me," he growled against the seam of my mouth.

He walked us out of the room, up the stairs, and into the first room. The room was empty except for a large bed with blue sheets beneath a huge window overlooking the whole town. He laid me gently down on the mattress. His body followed and laid over me, our mouths clashing once more. He moaned, and I closed my eyes, letting myself fall under his spell. Any chance of forcing him away was no longer possible, and I looped my arms around his neck and lifted my head to get closer, knowing I'd been yearning for this since we first met.

Rolling onto his side next to me, his hand traced down my jawline, over my collarbone. With a softness I hadn't known he was capable of, he ran his fingers over the tops of my breasts, teasing me. A growl rolled from his chest, and he smoothed his palm over my breast, my nipples so tight, so hard, they hurt in the best possible way. He squeezed and kneaded my breast as I kissed him deeply, squeezing my thighs together.

I craved him and begged for him to bring to life that insatiable feeling he'd brought out in me every time we crossed paths.

His fingers trailed over my ribs and found the line of bare skin between my top and shorts.

I moaned, refusing to give name to this urgency that I had to be with him.

He flipped open the button to my denim shorts, tracing his fingertips across the top of my underwear elastic.

My breath raced, and I held onto him tightly, ready and nervous at the same time. I'd only ever been with Alistair... and those weren't times I wanted to think about right now. Or else I wouldn't be able to do this.

"I won't hurt you," he murmured, as if he could read my mind. His mouth found the soft flesh under my earlobe. "Please?" he asked desperately, and relief drifted through my veins that he was asking for permission.

I nodded, unable to find my voice at first. Then I whispered, "Yes."

The smile he rewarded me with was filled with delicious promises I was desperate for him to keep.

He tugged my earlobe into his mouth as his fingers

slipped under the elastic of my underwear, sliding down to where I was soaking wet

When he found the entrance, he dipped his finger into me, sliding in and out, then he added another.

I cried out, chasing the feeling I was desperate for. Tilting my head back in the pillow, I moaned, my hips rocking with the movement of his fingers working in me as his mouth claimed the side of my neck, licking and kissing me.

If I could freeze time, it would be this moment...when I got lost in Wilder.

When he pulled free, I groaned with protest, and he gave a light laugh, clearly enjoying my reaction to him.

"You're going to be the end of me," he said softly as he pushed himself up. His gaze danced down my body, studying every inch of me and making me squirm.

"I'm going to claim you, baby. Imprint myself on your skin. After today, you'll never forget me."

I licked my lips, unsure how to respond when my initial instinct was to scream out, *yes*. As if sensing my eagerness, he bent forward, and in one swift move, he lifted my ass and yanked off my shorts and underwear. Pulling them off my legs, he tossed them aside, his eyes never leaving me.

"Show me everything. Take off your top," he ordered, a hint of his alpha power threading through his voice and only sharpening my lust.

To my surprise, I didn't hesitate and pulled the tank top up and over my head. When I went to unlatch the lace bra, he took my hand. "No leave it on." He reached over and tugged down the lacy cups, freeing my breasts. They bounced from his roughness. He grabbed one, squeezed it, and pinched my nipple. "Even more beautiful than I imagined," he said hoarsely.

There was something empowering about having someone like Wilder stare at me like I was the most incredible thing he'd ever seen.

He climbed back onto the bed, parting my legs, and positioned himself between them. I shifted to accommodate him. His gaze was riveted between my thighs, taking all of me in, and he smiled cockily like he knew he'd won.

Before I knew it, he leaned down, bowing before me, and his mouth latched onto my most intimate spot without a hint of hesitation.

"Oh my goddess." I arched my back as he licked me, his tongue taking short, fast flicks that drove me wild. The sounds he made, the savagery with which he ate me, left me panting for breath.

I'd never had a man go down on me, and his tongue was velvet against me. He groaned like a beast as his fingers prided my legs open wider.

My whole body tensed, goosebumps breaking out over my body, excitement building and building. I'd never felt this turned on.

I felt raw, exposed, but somehow, it didn't hurt like it had with Alistair.

My body was at the breaking point when he suddenly broke away. I lifted my head and looked at him like he was insane as he licked the glistening juices from his lips.

Holy shit, this man was hot.

"Why did you stop?" The air rushed out of my lungs so hastily that it left me dizzy.

The need and smile on his face told me he knew exactly what he was doing. "I can't give you everything you want so easily," he teased. That look crossed his face, the one where I could see he got pleasure out of making me squirm.

I narrowed my gaze at him and pulled myself to sit up, drawing my legs closed. He tsked softly.

"I'm nowhere near finished with you," he growled out, his hands on my knees, parting them again. "Stay like that for me."

I shouldn't have listened to him, but my sex fogged mind wasn't thinking logically. "You can be a real ass sometimes, you know that?"

He laughed, and damn him for making me love the way he sounded. He yanked off his shirt, throwing it behind him, then his hands fell to the belt on his jeans. He unbuckled it, then popped open the button on his jeans. In no time, he dropped them to the ground and stepped out.

I'd never seen a more delicious sight as I did now watching Wilder stand in front of me, palming his cock. I gasped at the size. That thing wasn't fitting in me. Alistair hadn't been well endowed at all, thank goodness, a lucky thing for me.

Wilder was muscles and smooth skin...perfection.

"Y-you're so big." The words spilled from my lips.

"Umm, thank you," he said with a laugh.

"It's not going to..." I glanced down my body and closed my legs, then back at him. "I mean, it's not the first time, but will it hurt?"

Another chuckle burst from his mouth as if he never expected me to ask such a question.

"It'll probably hurt a bit at first, but then I'll have you crying out for more. Open up for me, baby."

He was definitely a man used to getting his way, and while part of me toyed with the notion of ending this now just to make it clear he didn't control me, my words refused to come. My body was refusing to listen to my mind, because logic had nothing to do with this. What we had between us was pure animalistic, raw hunger.

His hands touched my knees, making me feel things I'd only read about in books, things I'd only imagined were possible. "Open for me," he repeated. "Don't make me ask again." He gripped my knees gently, pushing them wide as he crawled between them and over my body. His hands were pinned against the mattress on either side of my head.

I breathed heavily, enthralled with the feeling of him claiming me.

"I still hate you," I said suddenly, wanting him to know that while I wanted him badly, I still hadn't forgiven him.

"I hate you too," he said almost tenderly. But then his mouth was on mine, kissing me with unrelenting passion.

He knew exactly what he wanted and how to take it, and I was the prey to his predator. My body hummed beneath him. He leaned forward, my legs forced wider, his chest deliciously pressed against my breasts.

I tingled all over, my breath speeding up in anticipation.

"My gorgeous Rune, this makes you mine," he growled out as his erection pressed against my entrance, causing me to gasp in anticipation of his size. The tip of his cock was burning hot. He pressed his brow down to mine, our quickened breaths merging. "You ready?"

"Yes," I squeaked, my voice betraying me.

Finally, he pushed into me, taking it slowly, stretching me with his girth. My fingernails dug into his flesh.

"Scratch me, bite me, baby. Show me you want this. Do whatever you want, but I'm taking you hard today."

He pushed deeper into me as a deep-rooted groan came from my throat. He smirked, clearly loving my response.

The pain was there as he stretched me, but the pleasure was too.

"Let me in, sweetheart," he murmured.

"Wilder, please go slow," I choked out. I adjusted my hips slightly to better receive him. He moved deeper, until he was buried in me and we were one.

When he started to pull out and go back in, he fell into a rhythm. Slowly at first, as if getting me used to him, but it wasn't long before he moved faster, almost frantic in his movements. A groan vibrated against his lips when he kissed me.

The bed rocked, and our moans grew louder as they filled the room. I lost myself to Wilder, clutching him to me, my hips rocking to meet his. He pushed into me over and over, leaving me gasping in pleasure and knowing I would be feeling him for days after this.

A thundering growl escaped his lips. In this moment, he was truly the dominant alpha staking his claim. It was undisputable in his gaze.

I should've cared, but how could I when I felt like this? I wrapped my legs around his hips, clinging to him. He slid a large hand under my ass, lifting my hips slightly, going deeper within me.

My moans morphed into cries for more.

His mouth was on my neck, teeth grazing across my flesh. "I'm not ever going to let you forget you're mine," he said roughly.

Euphoria consumed me, a force so powerful, I stood no chance of making any kind of logical response. I moaned louder, my body tensing with the burning climax that was so close, I could taste it. He slid his hand between our bodies, his thumb finding my clit, and strummed it.

Whatever I thought I felt before was a warm up. The storm rolling over my body came at me so ferociously, so suddenly, I stiffened. It crashed through me, dragging me away. My heart thundered inside of me, and I dug my finger-nails into Wilder's shoulders, trying to ground myself.

Wilder groaned in response, his mouth parting, a moan sliding out. My heart clenched as I squeezed his cock, loving the pleasure on his face...pleasure I was causing.

I screamed as the orgasm continued. Wilder kissed me, stealing the sound, thrusting into me a few more times before following me over the edge with a long, tortured groan.

When his mouth finally broke from mine, I dragged in a heavy breath, half laughing, half wanting to cry at how insanely good that was. My lips felt bruised from how hard he kissed me, and my fingers were still lodged into his shoulders.

"I don't ever want to let you go," he told me, his words sounding like a declaration...a promise that I wasn't sure I wanted.

Collapsing back on the bed, I laid there spent, Wilder still buried inside me.

He slipped out of me, and I missed him instantly. That wasn't good.

He dropped onto the mattress right next to me and drew me into his arms, our bodies chest to chest, his leg looped over mine, caging me with his body.

Leaning into him, I let myself melt against his hard chest, my head cradled against him. The way he held me was primal and possessive, and everything about Wilder fell into that category. His body pressed against mine, and I found myself wanting him again.

He kissed the top of my head and made a satisfied groan that sounded dominating. "Stay with me," he ordered.

And for maybe the first time, I didn't want to argue with him.

His breathing slowed, and his heartbeat thumped comfortingly against my head. I melted against him, lost in a dream.

And for just one foolish second, I let myself believe in the possibility...of us.

*H*er head was on my chest, and I struggled not to shiver as she softly caressed my chest. I still couldn't believe what had just happened.

She was perfect.

Better than anything I could have dreamed.

I still wasn't sure how we'd ended up like this. When I'd lost control after I realized someone had hurt her, I'd fucking blanked. My wolf had risen to the surface, uncontrollable, intent on getting revenge.

I couldn't really blame it for going crazy. Rune had been driving me crazy since I'd first seen her.

There'd only ever been one other girl who'd triggered my wolf like this.

I didn't want to think about her with Rune still wrapped around me and her scent embedded in my skin. But I couldn't help it.

All this time, I'd been living like I'd lost the great love of my life. Arcadia wasn't my true mate, but she'd been mine. She'd been my first love...and I thought she would be my last.

I'd believed all this time that I would have to live dead inside, that I was never going to feel that spark light up my soul.

And then Rune had stormed her way into this town... into my life.

And everything had changed.

Wild. The word kept battering through my mind. I'd thought Arcadia was wild. There was always this desperate edge to her, like she didn't know if she'd see tomorrow. It made her the party girl, the one who sought out all the attention she could...the one that couldn't settle for one alpha when she could have two.

Arcadia was born a twin. Her brother had drowned in the creek when she was five and they'd been messing around by the river. He'd slipped on a rock and hit his head. Arcadia was too small to get him out of the water in time, and even a shifter couldn't regenerate from twenty minutes without oxygen.

Her brother's death had twisted something inside of her. Since the day he was put in the ground, she'd always been looking for something. And in my stupid, lust-filled teenage brain, I'd taken that desperation inside of her to be the wild I myself was desperate for. The one the elder had told me when I was a boy I would someday find.

I'd been a fool to ever think who I was looking for was Arcadia.

Because the wild in Rune...it was life-changing. It was the kind of wild you held onto, went anywhere with, did anything for.

It was the kind of wild I dreamed about. The kind I laid in bed and stroked myself to release just thinking about. The one I was addicted to and convinced that I couldn't live without.

The kind of wild I would do anything to keep.

I realized suddenly that her intoxicating touch had stopped, and there was a stiffness to her that was a far cry from the languid softness she'd been giving me just a minute ago.

"I need to tell you something," she whispered.

"You can tell me anything," I promised, sure that I meant it.

"I can't—" Her words halted, and her entire body shuddered against me.

"Tell me, baby. Whatever it is, we'll figure it out."

"I can't shift," she finally said, her voice even softer, and she lowered her gaze from me.

I laid there shocked for a moment.

"What do you mean you can't shift? You haven't had your first one, or no one ever told you what to do?" I questioned. She was a little late not to have shifted yet, but I'd met a few wolves who were late bloomers. It wasn't the end of the world, and I could help her.

She sat up, that fucking gorgeous hair of hers sliding down her body. I stirred and shifted, trying to get ahold of myself, since she was obviously embarrassed about this and I needed to take it seriously.

Rune shook her beautiful head, tears appearing in those eyes of hers that I couldn't get out of my head. "My wolf was taken from me. The alpha in my old pack did something to me, and I'll never be able to shift. They branded me…"

Her words trailed off. There was a faraway look in her eyes as she reached back and touched a section of unblemished skin on her back, agony written across her face like she was experiencing the pain all over again.

It took a moment for me to realize she was telling me she'd been literally branded. Like she was cattle. Hot rage tore across my vision, and I saw spots. I needed to control myself. I couldn't wolf out right now, not when she was opening herself up to me.

"Baby," I whispered, the word coming out more of a growl.

She shook a little.

It hit me then what had been done to her. It was something we'd been told around the campfire as little kids, a tall tale designed to keep us in line.

I'd never heard of it actually being done.

It sounded like those bastards had performed the *shakranda*. A ritual designed to keep a wolf from shifting, permanently. It would explain why the scar from the brand wasn't visible. It was because the magic of the curse settled under your skin, serving as a kind of barrier around the wolf, encasing it inside.

Only the most despicable kind of monster would even attempt such a curse.

The story came out of her then.

And maybe I was a monster too, because imagining that she had a true mate out there, it was more than I could take. A loud growl erupted from my throat, and she pushed away from me, fear in her eyes.

I tried to take deep breaths, but the jealousy was more than I could take. I looked down at my hands, not surprised to see that they were fully transformed into claws and the sheets I was gripping were shredded to pieces.

"I'm sorry," I panted as I tried to control myself. I continued to take deep breaths, and my hands began to transition back. I felt the fur that had sprouted on my back retract.

Rune was looking at me accusingly, and I felt like a failure.

"What was that?" she asked hoarsely.

I got back in the bed and crawled towards her, hating how she tensed her body like she wanted to run away from me.

"I can't bear the thought that you have a true mate out there. The idea that the moon goddess gave you to someone else when I know with every drop of blood in my body that you're mine."

Her gaze softened. "I don't belong to him." She pursed her lips almost forlornly, and I realized there was still something inside of her that loved the asshole. I wanted to tear the piece of him inside of her heart out and replace it with me.

Maybe I was just as much of a psychopath as her ex.

A thought hit me. I didn't know much about the curse, but I knew her alpha's blood had been placed somewhere on that brand before it was placed in the fire. It required an alpha's blood for the curse to be triggered.

Maybe I could undo it by ordering her to shift. Just like how we ordered our pups to shift at a certain age.

"I want to try something," I told her.

She eyed me warily.

I took her hand and stroked her soft skin, taking a second to just feel her against me.

"I'm going to try and trigger your wolf. I'll command you to shift just like we do when our pups are learning. What they did to you is triggered by an alpha, so maybe an alpha can dismantle it as well."

Her body stiffened again. She sat there so still and silent, it was almost like she was frozen.

"Do you think...do you think that could really work?" she asked, another tear sliding down her perfect face.

I faltered for a second, my stomach clenching as I

stupidly realized how much it was going to kill her if it didn't work.

I licked my lips nervously. I was a strong alpha. I knew that. I'd been around the country at various shifter events, and there'd never been someone who'd come close to me in dominance level...with the exception of Daxon.

But I didn't know anything about what I was about to try.

I stood up and slid on my jeans, not bothering to put on my briefs since hopefully, we'd be celebrating after this.

I rolled my shoulders backwards, letting my power build inside and flow through my veins until I could feel my wolf right at the surface.

"Shift," I barked, my voice unrecognizable from its usual timber as my power flowed out of me.

I watched as she shivered, my power licking at her skin.

But nothing else happened.

I tried again and then again, suddenly desperate. If this didn't work, she was going to be done with me. I just knew it.

"Stop," she finally cried out.

My chest was heaving from my attempts, my breath coming out in sharp gasps.

She wouldn't look at me, despair cloaking her, dimming all of her light.

Rune abruptly got up and began to gather her clothes. "I need to get back," she mumbled.

"Rune, baby. I'm..." My words died. Sorry didn't really cut this. What could I even say?

"I'll see you later," she whispered to me, standing at the door for a second. I sniffed the air, wondering why I could smell shame all over her.

And then she was gone.

What the fuck had I just done?

I'd acted without thinking. I never did that.

It was only later, hours after she'd left my bed, that I realized she'd never told me why her ex had done that to her in the first place.

RUNE

*N*umb. That's what I felt as I walked back to the inn.

I was too numb to cry. It was like I'd been encased in ice.

I knew better than to get my hopes up. I knew it. And yet, like the idiot I proved myself to be time and time again, I'd thought for a moment, things were about to change.

If it was as easy as an alpha telling me to shift, it probably wouldn't have required a spell to do it in the first place.

The brand under my skin seemed to be burning, just rubbing in my shame once again.

Wilder's power. It had been overwhelming. Far stronger than Alistair's was, that had been easy to see.

If I hadn't been Alistair's equal, I sure as hell wasn't Wilder's. Whatever was wrong with me wouldn't have mattered if I'd fallen for a human. But with Wilder being a shifter, and an alpha no less...

It was laughable.

Daxon's face filled my head, and I angrily pushed it away.

I was on my way up the stairs when Jim called out from behind me. I flinched, not wanting to face him but not having a choice.

"I'm so sorry to ask you for this, but I'm desperate. Carrie's not feeling well, the crew we usually use for catering somehow got double booked...goddess knows how that happens in a town as small as ours...but they've really screwed us over. We have a dinner we're supposed to deliver food to by six, and I have to stay here and tend the bar. Is there any way you can help?" His words rushed out, showcasing his desperation.

He acted as if nothing had changed between yesterday and today. I guess I could work with that.

"Whatever you need," I told him, forcing a smile. Regardless of the subterfuge, Jim and Carrie had helped me so much. I would probably do anything they asked of me.

Relief flooded Jim's features. "You're a gem, darlin'. I'll get everything loaded in the van and then I'll need you to get going right away."

"Of course," I told him. "I'm just going to run up and change, and I'll be right down."

I was suddenly aware that I must've reeked of sex, especially to a shifter. I was lucky Jim was kind enough not to mention it.

He nodded and rushed away, and I hurried up the stairs to change, wincing when I saw my reflection in the mirror.

I was a mess.

After I changed and did my best to clean up, I went down to the back of the inn, where Jim had loaded up the catering van.

I drove off, the urge to try and make a break for it hitting me hard. Right as I turned out onto the main road though, I saw two men I'd seen a few times with Daxon resting against a building on the far end of the road, a car by them, obviously on the lookout for me to probably do just that. By their presence, I had a feeling I wouldn't get far...

And after what had just happened with Wilder...I wasn't sure how far I even wanted to get.

I drove across the bridge and pulled up to the address Jim had given me. I examined the house, remembering what Wilder had told me about across the river being Daxon's territory. The house was a white-washed Spanish style, a little out of place with the other houses I'd seen around here. It also backed up to the woods.

There was no one up front, but Jim had said that the gathering was in the backyard, so I opened up the back and pulled out one of the trays of steak bites.

I hoisted it up and started around the side of the house where a path led through the trees. Hopefully, I could get someone to help me unload the rest when I got to the backyard.

Night was falling, and I shivered. I hurried my footsteps to try and find the party fast. The path seemed to go on forever. Where was the fucking backyard? Why couldn't I even hear anyone?

All of a sudden, a scream ripped through the air up ahead. I froze, not sure what I should do.

But the scream had kind of sounded...familiar.

Knowing I was a fool, I dropped the steak bites and raced ahead.

And then it was my scream filling the night.

Because Eve was lying there in the path, half of her neck missing.

She was dead.

The End

Star book 2, WILD HEART.

BOOKS BY C.R. JANE

The Fated Wings Series

First Impressions

Forgotten Specters

The Fallen One (a Fated Wings Novella)

Forbidden Queens

Frightful Beginnings (a Fated Wings Short Story)

Faded Realms

Faithless Dreams

Fabled Kingdoms

Fated Wings 8

The Rock God (a Fated Wings Novella)

The Timeless Affection Series

Lamented Pasts

Lost Passions

The Pack Queen Series

Queen of the Thieves

The Sounds of Us Contemporary Series (complete series)

Remember Us This Way

Remember You This Way

Remember Me This Way

Broken Hearts Academy Series (complete duet)

Heartbreak Prince

Heartbreak Lover

Ugly Hearts Series: Enemies to Lovers

Ugly Hearts

Academy of Souls Co-write with Mila Young (complete series)

School of Broken Souls

School of Broken Hearts

School of Broken Dreams

School of Broken Wings

Fallen World Series Co-write with Mila Young (complete series)

Bound

Broken

Betrayed

Belong

Thief of Hearts Co-write with Mila Young

Siren Condemned

Siren Sacrificed

Siren Awakened

Kingdom of Wolves Co-write with Mila Young

Wild Moon

Stupid Boys Series Co-write with Rebecca Royce

Stupid Boys

Dumb Girl

Crazy Love

Breathe Me Duet Co-write with Ivy Fox (complete)

Breathe Me

Breathe You

ABOUT C.R. JANE

A Texas girl living in Utah now, I'm a wife, mother, lawyer, and now author. My stories have been floating around in my head for years, and it has been a relief to finally get them down on paper. I'm a huge Dallas Cowboys fan and I primarily listen to Beyonce and Taylor Swift...don't lie and say you don't too.

My love of reading started probably when I was three and with a faster than normal ability to read, I've devoured hundreds of thousands of books in my life. It only made sense that I would start to create my own worlds since I was always getting lost in others'.

I like heroines who have to grow in order to become badasses, happy endings, and swoon-worthy, devoted, (and hot) male characters. If this sounds like you, I'm pretty sure we'll be friends.

I'm so glad to have you on my team...check out the links below for ways to hang out with me and more of my books you can read!

Visit my Facebook page to get updates. www.facebook.com/groups/C.R.FatedRealm

Visit my Website. www.crjanebooks.com

Sign up for my newsletter to stay updated on new releases, find out random facts about me, and get access to different points of view from my characters.

BOOKS BY MILA YOUNG

Shadowlands

Shadowlands Sector, One

Shadowlands Sector, Two

Shadowlands Sector, Three

Chosen Vampire Slayer

Night Kissed

Moon Kissed

Blood Kissed

Winter's Thorn

To Seduce A Fae

To Tame A Fae

To Claim A Fae

Shadow Hunters Series

Boxed Set 1

Wicked Heat Series

Wicked Heat #1

Wicked Heat #2

Wicked Heat #3

Elemental Series

Taking Breath #1

Taking Breath #2

Fallen World Series Co-write with C.R. Jane

Bound

Broken

Betrayed

Belong

Beautiful Beasts Academy Co-write with Kim Faulks

Manicures and Mayhem

Diamonds and Demons

Hexes and Hounds

Secrets and Shadows

Passions and Protectors

Ancients and Anarchy

Subscribe to Mila Young's Newsletter to receive exclusive content, latest updates, and giveaways. Join here.

ABOUT MILA YOUNG

Best-selling author, Mila Young tackles everything with the zeal and bravado of the fairytale heroes she grew up reading about. She slays monsters, real and imaginary, like there's no tomorrow. By day she rocks a keyboard as a marketing extraordinaire. At night she battles with her mighty pen-sword, creating fairytale retellings, and sexy ever after tales. In her spare time, she loves pretending she's a mighty warrior, walks on the beach with her dogs, cuddling up with her cats, and devouring every fantasy tale she can get her pinkies on.

Ready to read more and more from Mila Young? www.subscribepage.com/milayoung

Join my Facebook reader group.
www.facebook.com/groups/milayoungwickedreaders

For more information...
milayoungarc@gmail.com

Printed in Great Britain
by Amazon